Skank

Skank

Teresa McWhirter

James Lorimer & Company Ltd., Publishers
Toronto

James Lorimer & Company Ltd., Publishers acknowledges the support of the Ontario Arts Council. We acknowledge the financial support of the Government of Canada through the Canada Book Fund for our publishing activities. We acknowledge the support of the Canada Council for the Arts for our publishing program. We acknowledge the Government of Ontario through the Ontario Media Development Corporation's Ontario Book Initiative.

Cover Image: iStockphoto

Library and Archives Canada Cataloguing in Publication

McWhirter, Teresa,
  Skank / Teresa McWhirter.

(SideStreets)
Issued also in an electronic format.
ISBN 978-1-55277-716-9 (bound). — ISBN 978-1-55277-715-2
(pbk.)

  I. Title. II. Series: SideStreets

PS8575.W484S53 2011   jC813'.6   C2010-907412-2

James Lorimer &
Company Ltd., Publishers
317 Adelaide Street West,
Suite #1002
Toronto, ON, Canada
M5V 1P9
www.lorimer.ca

Distributed in the United
States by:
Orca Book Publishers
P.O. Box 468
Custer, WA USA
98240-0468

Printed and bound in Canada.
Manufactured by Webcom in Toronto,
Ontario, Canada in February, 2011.
Job # 375120

MIX
Paper from
responsible sources
FSC® C004071

To Ashley and Kathleen

Chapter 1

"It's none of your business, BITCH!"

"I'm MAKING it my business."

I'm jolted awake by two girls screaming at each other outside my window. I lie in bed, listening but not moving. It's a late August morning, and summer feels like it's barely hanging on.

"Get off my property!"

"YOU get off MY land!"

Their yelling is not enough to get me out of bed. I'm used to hearing loud people around here. Sleep is more important. I roll over and put the pillow over my head. But then someone starts banging on the front door and I jump out of bed.

"Mom?" I holler. No answer. "Mom, are you home?" The kitchen is empty and so is the living room. Downstairs in the basement apartment the two German shepherds won't stop barking.

I pull back the curtain to check who's knocking,

and it's a pissed-off looking Native girl, around my age. She's wearing a shirt that says *Ovary Action*, board shorts, skate shoes, and a faded denim vest covered in patches. Her long, black hair is curly and wild. Against my better judgment I take off the chain and open the door.

"Ummm, yeah?"

"Hey, sorry for knocking like the cops," she says. "But I thought you should know you have some real creeps living downstairs." It catches me off guard, though I'm not totally surprised to hear this.

The crusty French punks were already living in the basement when Mom and I moved here four months ago. They cram together in a surly bunch, with dirty caps and studded jackets. Mom went down and introduced herself after we settled in. I stayed upstairs and when she left I could hear them laughing at her. The scariest one is a skinny girl with messy dreads dyed a washed-out green. Their dogs are always barking.

"My name is Raven. Can I use your phone?"

Just then the skinny girl whips around the corner of the house. She's wearing combat boots and a dingy tank top. Her bruised, bony legs stick out of denim shorts. She comes to a screeching halt when she sees Raven and I talking. The girl glares at us then stomps across the yard and out the front gate. "Just wait until Ashtray gets home," she spits over her shoulder.

"Oh, what an anarchist you are," Raven mocks. "You're really gonna take down the government?

You can't even take care of your DOGS."

We listen to the girl rant down the street, until I'm left standing in my fuzzy pyjama bottoms. "What just happened here?"

"You should look downstairs."

I'm scared but curious, too. "Hold on, just let me change. Uh, I'm Ariel." I feel kind of awkward and close the door on her, then race to my room where I quickly pull on shorts and slip a bra on under my tank top.

When I come back Raven jokes, "I guess you don't leave the house without those tied down, eh?" It's a reference to my 38DD chest, and I shrug it off.

I lock the door and follow Raven past my mom's little garden in the front yard and the pitiful patch of grass for a lawn. Down the sloped path to the back with its scattered garbage, old tires, a mouldy couch with a lovely layer of mice droppings. Everything stinks. The German shepherds are going nuts.

Raven points to the window, and the barking gets even louder when I look inside. My stomach turns, and I understand why Raven's so mad. The dogs are chained to a metal table in the kitchen, and the floor is covered in dog shit.

I don't want to be here when Ashtray gets back.

* * *

We find the number for the SPCA and Raven calls. She has a soothing voice and sounds so adult when she talks to them. I wonder if she's Haida, with her

9

high, sharp cheekbones, but don't have the courage to ask. She sounds so calm on the phone, but her eyes are a furious blue-grey.

"They're gonna send an investigating officer to come and check it out," she says, hanging up. "You should call your landlord."

"Mr. Lee won't care," I scoff, "unless it involves collecting money." Raven nods knowingly.

Mr. Lee owns our rundown house and a couple of others, too. Since the rent is cheap, he doesn't think he has to do repairs. My mom gave up on landlords a long time ago and just learned it was easier to do things herself. Once I had to go to Mr. Lee's office to deliver rent. It was in a dusty old room at the back of a drugstore in Chinatown. He'd been playing video poker and stopped to look me up and down with greedy eyes. I never went back again.

"What grade are you in? I mean, do you go to school?"

I don't want Raven to leave. It's nice to have someone to talk to. I haven't made any friends in the neighbourhood. There aren't a lot of girls around here I'd want to hang out with. At least that's what I tell myself when I'm watching TV alone on a Friday night and even my mom has better things to do.

"I just need a few credits to graduate." Raven names the same school I'll be going to in September.

"That's where I'm starting grade eleven."

"It's a total shit-hole. The worst school ever."

"Awesome," I say. Raven giggles, and then we talk about the crusty punks downstairs, how only fucked up people mistreat their dogs. We agree we like animals more than most humans.

Raven tells me, "The only reason I went down there was to look for my sister Albertine. She's missing."

"Really?"

"She came down from Prince Rupert last month and was staying with my mom. Then she left to crash with friends. I keep missing her and leaving messages."

"Did you tell the police?"

"They won't file a report because she's twenty-one and has a history of running away."

We are silent for a moment, then Raven says, "Well, I'm going to check for her in Oppenheimer Park."

The park is only a few blocks down the street from my house, but it's not a place I go. Winos are always passed out on the grass, and homeless guys sleep on benches covered with newspapers.

But I'm lonely and bored. I ask, "Can I come too?"

* * *

After putting my hair in a ponytail and brushing my teeth, I grab my sunglasses and leave a note for my mom. It's welfare day, the last Wednesday of the month, so I figure she's gone to cash

11

her disability cheque and pay overdue bills. I open the fridge and mutter, close it, then open it again. Hopefully she's gone to get some groceries, too.

The sun is hot on the back of my neck as we walk. Today there is the rare, universal laughter of cheque day. Music blares out of random apartment windows. People bustle around buying food or new shoes or booze or crack or whatever. They seem relieved for a moment, even hopeful. Old guys gather on stoops, passing bottles wrapped in paper bags back and forth.

"Welfare Wednesday," I comment. "Good times."

"Only until tomorrow," Raven says. "Then comes Black-eyed Thursdays." I don't know if I should laugh, but I do.

We get to the park and there are some squeegee kids napping under a tree, a few parents with kids, and a solo woman walking her dog. A huge flock of pigeons peck at the grass. I'm surprised by the mellow scene. There's even a bench not covered in a homeless person. Raven walks over to ask two Native guys sitting on the grass about Albertine, then jogs back.

"Any luck?"

"Nope." Raven shrugs. "Let's keep walking."

I hesitate. "I shouldn't stay out super long. My mom will probably need some help when she gets back. If I'm not there, she does everything herself."

"What's wrong with that?"

"She's on disability," I tell Raven. "Her arthritis is really bad. Sometimes when it rains she can barely walk."

In truth, my mom doesn't let anything stop her, and will probably be glad that I was out of the house since I've been moping around all summer. "She's had it since she was a kid, but it got really bad about five or six years ago." *That's why we live down here now,* I almost say, then catch myself.

We walk down Hastings Street to Main, the centre of the poorest area code in Canada. The street smells like piss and is crowded with homeless people, drug addicts, and mental patients screaming at the sky. The junkies stumble around in traffic like shell-shocked zombies. One entire block is an open-air flea market, but everything is broken or dirty. A guy begs us for money, someone else tries to sell a stolen mountain bike, and we have to sidestep a woman lighting a crack pipe in the middle of the sidewalk.

This area is bordered on the west side by the downtown shopping district and the business centre, all expensive glass skyscrapers. On the east side is the industrial part of the city, with factories and a rendering plant that processes animal by-products. My neighbourhood is downwind from this, and some days the smell of rotten meat is unbearable. After a while you just get used to it.

Raven stops in front of one of the seedy old hotels and says, "My mom lives there."

"Oh." I take a quick look at a sick-looking person leaning in the doorway.

"Just wait here for a second," Raven tells me and disappears inside. I stand with my arms crossed over my chest. These hotels are SROs — single room occupancy — and the only places most people living in the Downtown Eastside can afford. Usually they are run by slumlords and have bedbugs. At least that's what I've heard.

Raven comes back looking annoyed. "My mom owes me twenty bucks, and she's not home."

"Do you stay here, too?"

"I live with my aunties." Raven names a social housing complex about eight blocks from where I live. "Do you get along with your mom?"

"She's pretty cool," I admit.

"What about your dad?"

"I can't really remember him."

It's a story often repeated, but I don't feel like telling it right now. Raven and I are both silent. I'm not sure what direction she'll take us in.

"Hey, let's go for ice cream," I say. Then I feel stupid, like an ice cream cone is really going to make Raven feel better about her mother, me about my dad, or make us forget those sick-looking dogs.

"I would," she says, "but I don't have any money . . ."

"I'll pay," I say quickly. We decide to go to the House of Gelato. It's a long walk, but they've got a thousand flavours. Criss-crossing through China-town—past the stalls selling dried fish and smelly squid, paper lanterns, panda bear keychains—we come to the industrial blocks of furniture ware-houses, auto body shops, and mattress factories. Random streets are blocked off to cars, and this is where the hard-looking daytime hookers stand. They size us up silently as we pass.

"Further down there is the kiddie stroll," Raven tells me.

"Kiddie stroll? What's that?" I imagine a picnic area filled with kids and balloons.

"It's where men go to get underage prostitutes."

"What? Really? Why doesn't someone tell the police so they can raid it or shut it down or something?"

"Duh," Raven says. "You think the police don't know?"

I say nothing and keep walking.

* * *

"Balsamic vinegar?"

"Ugh, garlic-flavoured gelato. Baaaarf!"

"Fennel," I say. "What's that?"

"It's an *herb*," the woman behind the counter replies, like I'm dense or something. When I ask for a sample, she seems annoyed, and I catch her staring at my chest before she looks away, embarrassed.

When I was twelve I developed practically overnight. Sometimes even *I* couldn't believe how big my breasts were growing. For years I hid them with baggy shirts and sports bras. Combine that with being a natural blond, and people automatically think I'm stupid. Also, some women will wrinkle their nose like they see something dirty or assume I'm some kind of slut. My boobs are a whole lot of attention I don't want. Besides the backaches, my posture is terrible from slouching over to hide them.

"Blue cheese!"

"Try the wasabi, Raven. I dare you."

"Only if you try the ass flavour."

This cracks us up. Finally, I decide on peanut butter chocolate, and Raven picks sour cherry. Outside we sit on the benches, licking our cones. It feels good with the hot sun beating down. Our fingers get sticky and Raven goes in for more napkins.

Around me are kids with ice–cream stained faces and weary parents. Couples stroll along holding hands. A guy sit-walking in a wheelchair beams at me as he rolls past. I'm taking in the scenery when an old classic Cadillac cruises slowly down the street and stops in front of me. The car is metallic green with fins, and the driver has sideburns and dark sunglasses. It seems like he's looking in my direction, but I can't be sure.

"What flavour is that?" he asks me.

"I'm not telling," I reply, and continue to lick.

The man laughs like I've told a hilarious joke. "What's your name?"

"Ariel," I say, smiling.

"I'm Julian. And you make that cone look real good." Just then Raven returns with napkins. "See you around," he says.

We watch him drive away. "Ugh. Creeper," Raven says. "How old is that guy? Was he hitting on you?"

"All I noticed was the car."

"Oh, so you're a tire-slut," Raven jokes. "Watch out, everyone! This one's – for dangerous."

This makes me laugh. It's been a pretty good day.

Chapter 2

When I get back, my mom isn't home yet. I can tell from the pill bottles on the counter and melting ice packs in the sink she's having another arthritic flare-up. I flip channels for a while and then hear her key in the lock. My mom comes limping in the door pulling her basket on wheels, and I get up to help her.

"Hey sweetie, I got some groceries. I found that cereal you like." She tries to heave a heavy bag onto the kitchen counter and grimaces.

"Mom, don't." I force it out of her hands. "Just relax. I would've come too, y'know."

"It's not easy to wake sleeping beauty," she laughs, then pulls out one of the kitchen chairs and sits down heavily.

"Is your hip still hurting?"

"It's okay, honey. Thanks for your help." She rubs her stiff leg as I open and close cupboard doors.

Then she gets up again and puts the kettle on for tea.

It's hard to keep my mom down. She's a small woman with kinky brown hair and laugh lines around her eyes when she smiles. I think they're beautiful. Growing up with a single mom means lots of freedom, and even though we might disagree or get annoyed with each other, the two of us never really fight. Even the time I did mushrooms with Dina and Tish and my mom caught on when we came home, instead of getting angry she made us pancakes and put on a trippy cartoon until we fell asleep. Everyone likes her. She's just a really nice lady.

"I think I made a friend today," I say. "While you were out this girl Raven knocked on the door and asked to borrow the phone, and then I went walking around with her."

My mom scans my outfit — short shorts and a breast-skimming tank top — but says nothing. Somehow I feel defensive. "She borrowed the phone to report the people below us. They totally mistreat their dogs, you know." She frowns when I tell her about what I saw downstairs.

"It made me sick," I say. "How can people live like that?"

My mom lets out a sigh. "I'll go and talk to those kids later," she says wearily.

"It won't do any good. Animal services are coming. Don't get involved."

Her joints creak as she stands. "What if everyone's attitude was, 'Why should I?' This world wouldn't be a nice place to live."

"But it's not anyway," I protest. My mom shakes her head and swallows a painkiller, then limps off to her bedroom to lie down.

I put the rest of the groceries away and wash a few dishes. Even though it's late afternoon and still hot, I slow-cook beans and chop vegetables for a chili dinner tonight. It hurts to see my mom in so much pain, and I wish things were better for her.

We once lived in a nice house in Kitsilano, just blocks from the beach. When the insurance money ran out, my mom had to sell it. That was the first of many moves, from the posh west side to east Vancouver. My mom had a hard time getting used to apartment living. She used to write for this music and lifestyle magazine but had to quit and go on disability. That's when we moved all the way down to the lower east side. She still goes into work one or two days a month to do copy editing and writes freelance articles from home. Mostly we live on her disability pension: $1,242.08 a month, with an extra $65 at Christmas. It's hard to adjust to not having things we once took for granted: a car, money for new clothes, buying what you feel like eating. Mom always says that money can't buy happiness, but it gives people the freedom to choose.

My stuff is all over the living room, mostly clothing and books, so I tidy up and start straightening the shelves. There's a portrait of my parents that makes me linger. My dad looks like a total old rocker, with long hair and a handlebar moustache, and he's laughing with his arm wrapped around my mom, who smiles up at him. I can't believe how young my mom looks. My dad, of course, never changes at all.

I stretch out on the couch and flip through the TV channels. My mind wanders to that guy Julian in the Cadillac, analyzes his degree of flirtation. Daytime TV is pretty pathetic, so I leave it on the video channel and stare mindlessly as three synchronized women bust out sexy moves in corsets and heels. It's hard to look tough while dancing in underwear. I get up and try a few of their unreasonable steps. The phone rings and I deep lunge for it.

"Hello?" I pant, already winded.

"Ariel, how *are* you?" It's my friend Dina. I can hear Tish in the background giggling. They've been my friends since elementary school. Both are brunettes, but Dina is short and bossy, and Tish is tall and athletic. Dina is the obvious brain, and Tish is the brawn. They call me the beauty or the boobs. It depends how nice they're feeling.

"I miss you guys." I can hear Tish laughing. "What are you two doing?"

Dina giggles. "I painted eyes on my chin, and oh my god, I swear that has kept Tish amused for hours."

"What's next? Seeing how she's affected by sock puppets?"

"Come over."

"I have to catch three different buses to get to your house," I sigh. "It takes forever."

"Cab it."

I don't bother saying I don't have the cash. They wouldn't understand. We've been close since third grade, and even when we moved from Kits to East Van, I was able to still go to the same high school. This year the district won't allow it.

"Why don't you guys come here?" In the four months I've lived on the lower east side, neither Dina nor Tish have visited. "Tish can drive. Or maybe you could come and get me."

Dina pauses. "Her mom won't let her take the car down there."

"Oh."

"Sorry."

I say, "It's not *that* bad here."

"Really?" There is an artificial brightness in Dina's voice that makes me think of a fluorescent light turned on.

"No. In reality I can smell dog shit, and I'm afraid of my neighbours."

"Grossies! Hold on, Tish wants to talk to you. She can't make up her mind about which look to go for on the first day of school. We can't even decide on footwear. It's *major*."

I settle in for a long, dull chat.

* * *

When my mom gets up, she has circles under her eyes. She thanks me for making dinner, and I can tell she's grateful. I'm happy I did something productive. The chili is spicy and I sprinkle grated cheese on top. We are silent as we eat. Then my mom says, "If you're nervous about next week, we can go take another look at the school."

I blow on a spoonful of chili. "Who said I'm nervous?"

"Are you?"

"Yeah," I admit.

"Sweetie, I know you had some problems at your last school. Maybe this year you should focus more on your studies."

I play dumb but know what she means. At least I think I do, but I don't want to ask. Mom says I'm a little too boy-oriented sometimes.

"Instead of what?" My voice rises. "It sounds like I'm being *accused* of something."

"Of course not, honey. Pass the margarine, please." One thing about my mom is that it's hard to get her into a fight. She'll just sit calmly and throw out facts.

"You mean because I failed Algebra last year? I'm not good with numbers, you know that. And it's the first class I've ever had to take again. Math has always been my worst subject. Even if you drill a concept into my head, it doesn't stick." It's true. I'll watch the teacher's lips move, but it's all dead air.

I stand up and start stacking dishes. "Ariel, you're a smart girl," my mom says. "Don't waste your time with distractions. Not all male attention is good."

"Says the woman who hasn't had a date in ten years."

As soon as the words come out of my mouth I'm horrified, but they can't be shoved back in. My mom gets up from her chair and walks to the bathroom, closing the door. I hear the bathwater running and the radio on loud.

It's true my mom never yells, but she did hit me once. It happened in the spring about a year after my dad was gone. My grade two teacher, Ms. Marsh, had chosen me to erase the blackboard after school. It was a coveted job because Ms. Marsh was pretty and gave out mints, and sometimes her boyfriend picked her up on a motorcycle. After school I chattered to Ms. Marsh and erased the blackboards, jumping to reach the high chalk marks. I told her there were rabbits living in my backyard and that I had a brand new baby brother named Rex who slept in my room. Ms. Marsh smiled like an angel as I lied.

That Saturday afternoon I was with my mom while she did errands, and afterwards we were going to Granville Island to get donuts and feed the ducks. She had bought fabric or something when Ms. Marsh saw us in the parking lot behind the store. "Congratulations on your new baby, Mrs. Stark," Ms. Marsh said excitedly. There was a bad look on my mother's face. One side of Ms. Marsh's mouth stopped smiling.

"Go wait by the car," my mother hissed at me. "And don't move." She didn't say a word on the way home, then pulled me into her bedroom. Oily jars of cosmetics knocked against each other on

24

the vanity as my mother spanked me with her heavy silver brush. I had never been hit before, and afterwards lay weeping on the bed. She said, "Don't ever tell lies about your father or me. I hate a liar more than anything."

A few dull thuds from downstairs snap me out of my thoughts. As I finish the dishes, I gaze out the side window. Shadowy figures move back and forth from the alley. The dogs are barking again downstairs, and I wonder if it's Ashtray, if they'll blame me for reporting them. It scares me to think he might do something to me or my mom. I hold my breath and wait. After the sounds of scraping furniture and more barking, there is the slide of a van door and tires screeching.

I go out onto the steps and hear nothing. Peeking around the side of the house, I see the lights are off, and their door is wide open. Everything is gone: the table, the posters, the dogs. Only their garbage remains. It's a relief, but then I feel bad, wondering about those dogs. I doubt they're going to a farm or even a place with a yard.

This is how problems are dealt with on the lower east side. People vanish.

Chapter 3

My high school is an ugly sprawl of cement. Right beside it is a huge park, and over the summer I saw kids here drinking and hanging out. Now there's a fence around the entire park for the next year as the city tears it down for redevelopment into a more "family-friendly space." At least that's what they've posted between the No Trespassing signs.

High school reminds me of the prison shows I've seen on TV. Everyone hangs out with like-minded people who look the same, and they travel in packs to protect their weakest. On the front steps, I squeeze through some guys standing in a clump and scoping out girls.

"Helloooo," someone says.

I go to the bathroom and check my appearance, add more gloss to my lips. I'm pretty sure I look good. I've got new ankle boots my mom splurged and bought for me, designer jeans we found at a thrift store, and a scooped necked white t-shirt. My long blond hair took an hour to straighten this morning, but falls in a shiny wave down my back. I clutch my books to my chest and walk into homeroom. A group of skateboarder jock types have taken over the back desks. One points at his lap and says to me, "Hey, why don't you come and sit here?"

"Dude! Nice one."

"Haw haw!"

This is my trick for being in awkward social situations: I plaster a smile on my face. Refuse to stare at the floor or show fear. Even if inside is all panic and terror, I remain outwardly composed. If they know something bothers you, it makes it so much worse.

I choose a seat in the front and drop into it slowly, the smile still on my face. Someone in the back whistles. After arranging my notebook I pretend to start writing, then take a quick glance around. Across the room, a black-haired girl with white streaks down the sides is glaring at me. She whispers furiously at the girl sitting behind her without taking her eyes off me. Both of them look pissed off.

Oh shit, I think.

* * *

It turns out my assigned locker is two away from the boy who whistled at me. He turns his ball cap backwards and hangs on the edge of his locker

27

door. "Hey, your name is Ariel, right? I remember from roll call."

I nod and look over. He's got a goofy smile on his face. "Ariel," he says. "Kiiiiller. I'm Jesse." He reaches out to shake my hand. Sandwiched between us is a tiny Vietnamese girl with glasses who shuts her locker and hurries away.

I ask him for directions to the biology lab and then one of his friends tells him to hurry up. "Forget it," Jesse says. "I'm talking to Ariel."

I spin my lock shut. "Don't worry, I'll find it." Then I realize my shirt has fallen off my shoulder, exposing my black bra strap. Jesse's staring like it's a cobra about to strike. I yank my sleeve back up.

"Bye, Ariel," Jesse says, wiggling his fingers in an exaggerated manner. Just then the skunk-haired girl from homeroom walks by with another friend.

"Ariel?" she snorts. "More like Areola!"

"Ah hah! Kat, that's hilarious!" says her friend. They screech down the hallway. I look at Jesse.

"Uh . . ." he stammers, then laughs and slouches away.

My first day, and I already have a nickname.

* * *

I look around for Raven in the cafeteria but don't see her. For the next hour, I try to pretend I enjoy listening to people talk and laugh around me. In my head I try to calculate if it's possible to travel home every day for lunch. Then Jesse walks by with his friends and says, "Hey, Ariel, come with us."

Anything is better than sitting alone. I follow the boys outside and climb through a hole in the back of the fence around the park. It's where they go to sneak smokes. I am introduced to Fat Joey, the joke being that he is very tall and skinny, and some guy called Mink who has way too much facial hair to be in high school. Jesse asks me, "Where was your last school?"

"Charles Tupper," I say.

The guys make some cracks about sluts they know from Tupper, then change the joke to Surrey girls. The bell rings and they swagger back inside while I follow behind.

After lunch I have English, which is always my best class. Our teacher gives us an assignment to write down a happy memory. I start mine by saying my mom has a degree in Literature and I have to sneak vampire novels into the house. My happy memory is going to the big downtown library, the one that looks like a Roman Coliseum, and afterwards buying a bag of green grapes that we share sitting on the couch while reading our books together. My teacher gathers the papers and reads out a bunch of them, including mine. When she gets to the end, she says it's lovely and gives a sigh.

* * *

After school I hang around the library a bit, flipping through books. It almost seems like it's going to be an easy semester: along with Earth Science and English, I have French 11 and Textiles. At least for right now I don't have to deal with my dreaded Algebra class.

I walk out the front doors. Right away I see that girl Kat with a group of her friends at the bottom of the stairs. There's no other direction to go. I keep walking, feeling eyes on my back. Then I hear footsteps rush up, and before I can turn around someone shoves me. I trip and regain my balance. It's Kat, chest heaving and teeth bared.

"Stay away from Jesse, whore."

"I barely know the guy!"

"Bullshit! You think you can come to *my* school and start flirting with *my* boyfriend? You better watch yourself."

"He never said he was your boyfriend." Right away I should've known about Jesse. Boys like him are always trouble.

"Her and Jesse broke up," another girl informs me. By now I'm swarmed with them. "But they're gonna get back together."

"So keep your big tits away from him," Kat warns.

"She loves to walk down the hall and jiggle her boobs," someone says. I open my mouth to protest when Kat swings her purse and clocks me on my left ear. My books fly out of my hands and I grab the side of my head. It hurts.

"Leave me alone," I say, but it doesn't sound very forceful. There are a couple of other kids standing around, but no one does anything.

"You leave Jesse alone. Got it, Areola?"

They say a few more nasty things as they walk away that get drowned out by the ringing in my ear.

* * *

I walk down Commercial Drive, past the Italian delis and pastry shops, hemp stores blasting reggae. My hand clenches my ear, and I fight back tears of embarrassment and rage, going over and over what just happened.

The problems started back in sixth grade when I got my boobs. Kids would laugh at the way they bounced in gym class. Boys snapped my bra strap or drew cartoons of me on the board before class. I've always been taller and looked older than other kids my age. Then, when I was thirteen and starting high school with Dina and Tish, the older boys gave me lots of attention. After a lot of parties and drinking and hookups, I realized it was just easier to be with one person. Dina and Tish like to say that I get around, but I've only slept with my two exes, despite what everyone thinks. But if people decide you're a slut, you get stuck with that label forever.

My ear thuds with pain. I'm mortified at the thought of telling my mom what happened at school. Not only am I humiliated, but now I'm pissed off, too. People are out there in the world doing a lot worse things than me, yet I always seem to be dumped on. I knew it was going to be a tougher school, but it's only the first day and already more horrible than I imagined. There isn't a smile on my face anymore.

* * *

Before I open the door to my house, I comb my hair down over one side so it covers my swollen ear. I walk in and hear voices in the kitchen. A familiar figure sits at the table with my mom. "Uncle Jack," I say, and swoop down to give him a big hug. Then I grab a cigarette from his pack.

"Well, hey there! If it isn't the prettiest seagull I've ever seen."

"Ariel, put that back," my mom says. "You know I don't like you to smoke."

I pretend not to hear her. "How long are you staying, Uncle Jack? Is Aunt Cathy with you this time?"

"Unfortunately, I'm just passing through. She sends her love."

Uncle Jack isn't really my uncle, but I've known him since I was born. He was my dad's best friend, and runs a merchandise company in New York that makes t-shirts for bands. He and his wife Cathy always send me cards with money for my birthday and graduation, and there's a big stack of presents from them every Christmas.

"How did it go today, Ariel?" My mom got up this morning to make me cinnamon French toast. She knew I was nervous about my new school.

"Great," I say quickly. "So, are we going to

the Spaghetti House tonight?" Uncle Jack always takes us there when he's in town. It's still decorated in orange and brown from the seventies, and the back room is full of ancient Italian men who look like old mobsters.

"You bet, kiddo."

"Ariel, I need to talk to Jack. Can you give us a minute, please?"

I look back and forth at them, then get up. On the way to my bedroom Uncle Jack says, "She looks more grown-up every time I see her . . ." I close the door on *that* conversation.

On my bed is a small box with the logo from a phone company, and there's a cellular inside. The phone is razor thin and pink, but I know already my mom probably won't let me keep it. Over the years Uncle Jack has tried to help us more, but she's got a lot of pride. Usually, if it's something I really want, she'll cave in.

"Is this for me?" I ask, coming back into the kitchen and waving the phone.

"We're discussing it," my mom says.

"All the kids at school have one."

"It's not something you *need*. I don't believe kids your age need to be walking around with phones stuck to their faces." My mom is so old-fashioned when it comes to technology. We have a computer, but it's an old one someone gave us and the connection is super slow. *Kind of like her,* I think, and then feel bad. "And besides," my mom continues, "you have to sign up for a plan and then you're locked into some evil corporation." I let out an exasperated sigh.

"It's pre-paid for six months," Uncle Jack says, and I could kiss him. "Karen, it's also about her protection. This is not the safest neighbourhood for a teenage girl."

My mom bristles. "I would never endanger my daughter. Just because it's lower-income housing doesn't mean she can't leave the house safely. The people in this neighbourhood have been marginalized for years, Jack. There's a very strong sense of community here. Stronger than most people would like to think."

"What if there's an emergency at school? Do you want her to spend time looking for a pay phone and finding correct change?"

That's the one that wins her over.

* * *

Before we hit the Spaghetti House, Uncle Jack takes us for a ride in his rented car. He used to keep a second home in Vancouver, but he sold it a few years ago during the housing boom. My mom and Uncle Jack talk in the front seat as he takes little detours. We pass the lineup at the gospel mission that snakes all the way around the block. Working girls shimmy in bikini tops and thigh-high boots. A man jerks back and forth across the street. In an empty lot there are a few makeshift shelters, and someone has scrawled TENT CITY on a big piece of cardboard. There's an overlap between our area and Gastown, formerly known as old Cracktown, which has been renovated over the last few years and is now a pricey tourist area, full of expensive boutiques and martini bars. Uncle Jack is astonished by the rapid construction.

At the restaurant we order plates of spaghetti and garlic toast. After the salad comes, I excuse myself and head to the washroom. While walking through the restaurant, I make eye contact with a familiar-looking man with a pompadour. He sits cozy in a booth with a woman wearing a tight dress and too much makeup. I recognize him. Julian, the flirtatious guy in the Cadillac from outside the House of Gelato. The way he is staring makes me blush. His date notices too and slams her hand on the table. Julian just laughs at her. It's an ugly sound. I make sure to stay in the bathroom so long that when I come out they're gone.

"Your food is getting cold," my mom points out when I finally make it back to the table. After the spaghetti, we all share a thick slice of cheesecake, and she asks if I'm ready for school tomorrow.

I groan, "I'm in a happy food coma. I don't even want to consider it right now." One look at my mom and she can tell I'm holding back. "Okay, I might have pissed off the wrong girl today, just because her boyfriend talked to me." I know there's the option to be home-schooled, or try some alternative program. But there's a part of me that refuses to be bullied. If I let every jealous girl dictate my life, I may as well go ahead and get my breasts reduced, too.

"Fight back," Uncle Jack advises. "Even if you just scratch their eyeball, it'll make them remember, and they'll pick on someone weaker next time."

"Jack!" my mother says. "That's terrible advice. Did you learn that in prison?"

It's nice to hear her laughing. I wonder if it's hard for my mom to see Jack sometimes, and all the memories it brings up. Or maybe she needs that connection to my dad and the past, but it's hard to love a ghost.

Chapter 4

I don't see Raven until the second week of school. My favourite class is Textiles, because I can sit at my sewing machine alone and time flies past. Now Jesse talks to me in a grand, exaggerated manner I can tell is just for show. If I wasn't already screwed up, it might give me a complex or something.

The final bell rings and the hallway fills with kids. When I get to my locker I see someone has crammed a note in the side of the door. I fling it over my shoulder without looking at it. Down the hall I can hear some girls snickering, but I don't bother to turn around. It's Katrina Kubalowski, otherwise known as Kat. I wish Katrina Kubalowski would die. Die! I force myself not think about her. Hate tastes sour in the bottom of my mouth.

I'm leaving the building out the back door when I hear someone call, "Ariel!" It's Raven. She breaks away from a couple of kids and jogs over.

"Hi, Raven! I kept hoping I'd run into you."

"My only classes are Drama and Native Studies," she says. "It's great. I never have to be here. You heading home?"

"Yeah," I say, and Raven falls into step beside me. She's wearing her denim vest, and her hair is in two thick, glossy braids tied with cords of white leather at the ends.

"This place sucks, eh?"

"Sure does," I say.

"Don't worry, it's bound to get worse."

This makes me laugh. As we walk, I notice two girls sitting on a bench watching me.

One says to the other, "Oh my gawd, can you believe that girl? She's the one that I heard got a boob job."

Her friend sneers. "They don't even *look* real."

They must think I can't hear them, or maybe they don't care. My face turns red with embarrassment.

Raven stomps right up to them. "You know what? They ARE real. And you two are just jealous 'cause you're a couple of MUTTS."

Their mouths drop open and we walk on in perfect time.

* * *

"I still haven't found Albertine," Raven says as we share a plate of fries in a cheap diner. "Even my mom is getting worried." She rips open another package of ketchup, and it spurts onto the plate.

"Where's the last place you saw your sister?"

"With the Kitkatla band, on Dophin Island. It's right by Prince Rupert. We used to be really close. We both have wolf names."

I'm intrigued. "What's your name?"

"Kuukh Bam Yaw. It means, 'The wolf that goes ahead of the pack for food.'"

"You're a wolf," I say. "That's so cool. How do you get given a name like that?"

"Our mom is Cree, from the plains, so she had her wolf passed down to us. It's a matrilineal society; everything goes through the mother," Raven explains. "So I'm Wolf, even though I'm Tsimshian and part of the killer whale tribe. They had an adoption ceremony."

"What was the ceremony like?"

"My sister and I were scared. All the elders sat around discussing us. It was weird to have all these people we didn't know talking about us in a language we didn't understand."

"I don't have a culture," I say. "I'm boring and white."

"It's all mayonnaise," she laughs. "Except for you."

"I'll help you look for Albertine. I'll be your sidekick or something like that."

"Great," Raven says. "We can meet everyday after school." A huge sense of relief floods over me.

We finish the fries and decide to walk down to Crab Park. It's a thin slice of sand surrounded by oil-slick water, also known as Rat Beach. There's no one here except some bearded, barefoot people with giant backpacks and camouflage pants who look like they've been living out in nature too long. We step over some logs and find a place to sit.

"Watch out," Raven warns me. "People leave their rigs in the sand."

Across the harbour loom the blue mountains of North Vancouver. Further down is Canada Place and the Convention Centre, where the gigantic cruise ships dock. A Seabus churns past, followed by a tugboat. There is a stench of the port and huge orange cranes loading and unloading containers of cargo. A few ducks paddle and quack, and I smell salt in the air beneath all the grime.

We aren't there long when Raven's leg starts tapping and she's restless. "I'm ready to go," she says, standing. "Let's go hit some pawnshops with a flyer." We walk down to Pigeon Park, this little slab of concrete for hustlers and junkies. I'm surprised when Raven says hello to a few of them. Inside the pawn it smells like foul body odour. I flip through a box of used CDs while Raven holds up a picture of Albertine to the owner.

"Have you seen this girl?"

The man is grey-haired and overweight, with thick glasses. His eyes flick over the photo. "Nope," he says.

"Her name is Albertine. She's twenty-one."

"I said I ain't seen her."

"Can I put up this poster?"

"No room."

"But you've got all these other notices up," Raven protests.

They bicker back and forth. I tune them out and lean over the front counter which holds a display case full of knives. Then the owner moves in front of me and asks, "There something you wanna see?" My skin crawls and I straighten up at once when I realize he's looking down my shirt.

I'm about to tell him off when I see Raven's worried face and decide to change tactics. "Come on," I say. "It's her sister and she's missing." I give him my best and brightest smile.

"Well, I guess it's alright. But just one," he grumbles.

Down the street is a country and western bar. Raven doesn't even pause at the door and just walks in. No one stops us. The bartender has thin lips and a sore on her chin. She scowls at the picture Raven shows her. "Never seen her," she says. We order cokes and the bartender squints at our faces, then brings two cans.

A sagging brunette with bad skin comes over to us. "Hey, Cokey Flo," Raven says. "This is my friend."

The woman chirps a greeting. There is a too-bright look in her eyes. She tugs at the scarf around her neck and then begins rambling. "I don't have a pedigree. But when I'm doing this good-girl thing and I'm being accused of bullshit, it's ugly. They're putting bugs in my house, I'm sure of it."

Raven asks, "Have you seen Albertine anywhere?" Cokey Flo drifts off, muttering.

We finish our cokes and sudden loud voices from the back make us turn in our seats. I'm shocked to see that Cokey Flo is lying splayed across the floor. "He HIT me," she bleats, pointing to two lumber-jack-looking guys playing pool.

"She was probably mouthing off," the bartender shrugs. "Those guys are my friends."

"CALL THE FUCKING COPS!" Flo screams. Raven tries to help her up and she thrashes wildly. Other patrons just sit and watch.

"You girls better get out of here," the bartender warns.

* * *

At home there's a note from my mom on the table saying she's at a doctor's appointment. My heart is still racing from the encounter in that horrible bar. I can't get over how everyone just stood around staring, even though there was a woman lying on the floor with a bleeding head. I call Dina, but it goes right to voice mail, so then I try Tish, who answers.

"Hey," I say, "I had a really weird day." Then I tell her about Cokey Flo.

"Oh my god," Tish says. "I'm going to pray for all those poor people." When Tish's parents separated last year, her mom started going to church and dragging Tish with her. At first Tish resisted, but then her mom got crazy about religion, the kind where you go to church twice on Sundays.

Even though her dad moved back in the house, sometimes it's like Tish has been absorbed by a cult or something.

"Thanks. I'm sure your prayers will really help." The sarcasm goes completely past her.

"Oh, did I tell you I got an iPhone? It has all these apps, and I have one that shows me what I'd look like if I were styled like different celebrities. There's one that even —"

"I have a cell phone now, too," I interrupt. "How come you never call me?"

"Sorrrrry," Tish says. "Me and Dina are just so busy this year with volleyball and the spring musical." Then she starts going on about her new phone again.

It's funny how you can talk to someone who's supposed to be one of your closest friends and they feel like a stranger. Dina and Tish don't even know about Raven, that she's a tough girl who's got my back. And she's got the kids at the Native youth centre behind her. Sometimes I look around school at the different groups, how everyone sticks together. It may be a UNICEF Club or the Grad Council or a goth band of misfits, but there will be others the same. I have never felt that way. Even with Dina and Tish, I was always the odd one out.

The only good thing about being ignored at school is that with no distractions, I get better marks. I want a scholarship so I can go to a school far away. My secret fear is that geography won't change a thing, and the rest of my life will be as awful as it is now. My entire lame social life consists of doing my homework in the library. With two more years ahead of me to go, I feel like yanking my hair out in frustration.

* * *

It's Friday afternoon, and I bang my locker shut. It's such a relief having two whole days away from this place without enduring whispers and dirty looks. There must be some new rumour going around. I've seen people actually point me out in the hallway. Raven is in our meeting spot at the bike racks. As usual, her restless leg is tapping, tapping. "Hey, are you going to the show tonight?"

"What show?"

"Juvenile Hall."

I shrug nonchalantly. Not only have I not heard about it, I don't even know the band she's talking about. "I'm not sure."

"They're playing an all-ages show. You should come."

"Maybe," I say.

"We can have some drinks and go together if you want."

"Okay, cool." I'm beginning to feel like this could be an exciting night. I can't remember the last time I did anything fun.

"I'll have to stop by my mom's," Raven says. "She'll get some booze for us." We make a plan to meet later, and I practically bounce all the way home.

After dinner I shower, then blow-dry my hair and curl it. I'm in the middle of applying make-up when my mom comes into the bathroom. I'm wearing a black dress that shrunk in the wash and is pretty tight on me, patterned stockings, and my favourite ankle boots.

"What kind of concert is this?" she asks.

"Don't worry, I'm wearing a denim jacket over-top."

"That's not what I asked."

"Mom, it's the usual kind of all-ages show. Don't worry, I'll be with Raven." She's stopped by a few times, and I know my mom really likes her.

"Will there be any drinking?"

I level my gaze at her in the mirror. She knows I won't lie.

"Don't worry, I'll be responsible," I say. "I promise."

My mom just gives me a sad, knowing look.

* * *

My meeting spot with Raven is at a buck-a-slice pizza joint. "Holy hot stuff," she says as I slide onto a stool beside her.

"Did you get the booze?" I'd already given her my last ten dollars, but my mom slipped emergency cab fare in my pocket.

"She wasn't home. Can I use your phone?" Raven punches in the number and drums her fingers while it rings. "MOM!" she says. "You were supposed to be home an hour ago. Remember, I asked you about the stuff for tonight?" Raven listens for a minute then says, "Okay," and snaps the phone shut with a frown.

"No luck?" I ask.

"We have to wait twenty minutes," she says.

"Are you hungry?"

"Yeah, but I'm flat broke."

The pizza boy looks our age and has bad acne on his face. I go to the counter with a handful of change, and smile as he counts the quarters and dimes. "You're twenty cents short for a slice."

"Oh, no," I say, picking up my coins only to put them down again slowly. "Sorry about that." Then I open my coat and push up against the counter. "Would it be okay if I brought the money in next time?"

"Don't worry about it," the boy stammers. "What kind do you want?"

"Really? Thank you so much! I *love* you."

I come back to the stool with a gooey slice of extra toppings. Raven shakes her head in disbelief. I'm in a great mood, excited and giddy. It feels like forever since I've been out. We pick at the pizza while watching people stream past the window. Everyone's at their Friday night finest. There's a feeling of adventure, of action, and the streets move fast: skinny guys in track suits on the hustle, wide-eyed tourists clearly lost, drug dealers passing off flaps. Everyone fights for their own little corner, and between it all, police cars cruise like silent white sharks.

As we walk out onto the street, I feel eyes on me. "Up? Down?"

"Hash," someone hisses.

"Oxys," says another.

At the hotel where Raven's mom lives, there's no buzzer at the door. It's dark in the entranceway and doesn't smell very good, like urine and black mould. We go up three flights, and someone comes out of the shared bathroom down the hall. They see us and scurry back to their room.

A woman answers the door in a tattered silk robe. "Get in and don't say anything," she whispers in a mushy voice, and yanks Raven inside. "He's still here."

"Mom, meet Ariel. Ariel, this is my mom, Annette."

"Netti," she says. Raven looks just like her, and I can tell Netti used to be a beautiful woman. They have the same black hair, strong nose, and sharp cheekbones, only Netti's eyes are deep, dark orbs. Her face sinks without dentures, and her collarbones jut painfully. Netti waves her arm at me and rushes back to the bedroom.

"There was a bedbug infestation down here last year," Raven whispers.

"Oh my god." I suddenly get paranoid that I'm sitting on the couch, but if I stand up I'll feel like a jerk.

"You have to get a new mattress and wash all your clothing and then have your place sprayed. So there was this whole epidemic, and do you know what the government did? They gave everyone an extra twenty bucks on their welfare cheques to deal with it. Can you imagine? Having bedbugs and never being able to get rid of them?"

I shudder. Then Netti comes out of the bedroom with her dentures in. A thin gold necklace glitters around her neck. She takes a bottle of vodka out of the cupboard and hands it to Raven.

"So you girls are going to a party? I like to party." She lights a smoke and cackles. It's easier to understand her with her dentures in, and she looks better, even though in her skinny jeans and tube top I can see the vertebrae in her spine. Her arms are so thin the bones stretch away from the skin.

"We know," Raven says. "Thanks for the bottle."

"Stay and have a drink," she says, as a man comes out of the back room. He grabs Netti by the hair and pulls her head back, gives her a vicious kiss. Netti cackles louder and throws up her arms. It's starting to dawn on me that she's high.

"Yeah, why don't you girls stay?" The man is not wearing a shirt and his gut sticks out in a hard potbelly. He's staring right at me. "We could have a real good time."

Raven stands up in disgust. "We're LEAVING."

* * *

The show is down some rickety stairs at a place called The Sweatshop. The band is three girls playing loud punk rock, but they've got pretty voices and sing delicate harmonies, too. The drummer has white-blonde hair that she whips around behind her kit, and the singer is this cute little maniac with a side ponytail jumping around in Spandex as she sings:

> *It's on your face and in the mirror*
> *You couldn't make it any clearer*
> *What did they teach you in school?*
> *Not much, not much . . .*

Raven and I rock out right in front, and she shoves the guys away who try to slam into me. The singer keeps looking down in our direction and giving us the thumbs-up. Raven and I sneak the bottle back and forth for quick sips of vodka. Every burning swallow makes me shudder, even though it's mixed with cranberry juice. Finally the set ends and everyone screams approval. I'm so sweaty my dress is stuck to me, and the air is hard to breathe. "Let's go outside," Raven says, linking arms to fight our way up the stairs. As we step into the cool night, I'm starting to feel really drunk. The flashing lights of a cop car blind me and I freeze.

They've got a kid facedown on the cement, with his hands pinned behind him. A cop kneels on his back and the kid yelps in pain. He only looks about thirteen years old and is fighting back tears.

"Get off him!" Raven screams right in their face, and the other people in the crowd start murmuring.

"You have to respect the charter of human rights!" I've never seen anyone act that brave. Then another squad car pulls up with the lights flashing.

"YOU WANT US TO BRING YOU IN, TOO?" a cop threatens. I'm positive they're going to arrest her, but Raven raises her hands. We fall back and melt into the shadows on the street.

"You've got to pick the right battles," she says.

Chapter 5

Despite a slight headache the next morning, I feel great. It's Saturday, and my mom has let me sleep in. After a veggie scramble and a shower, we take the bus to the big public library. The whole afternoon is spent reading and browsing, and finally we check out our stack of books. My mom takes me to a café nearby for hot chocolate, and we watch the people bustle by with shopping bags. It's early October and smells like smoke in the air.

"This was always your dad's favourite time of year," my mom says. "The touring would wind down during winter, and then we'd spend the next few months in front of the fire."

"We don't have a fireplace anymore," I point out. My mom pulls her scarf tighter. She's got her cane out today, so I know her hip must be hurting. And then I ask her, "Don't you ever want to be in love again?"

"You just summed it up, Ariel," she says. "I don't have a fireplace anymore. That part of my life is over."

But it doesn't really seem like it bothers my mom at all. There's a half-smile on her face, like she's remembering my dad and the good times they used to have. And I really admire her for that. It's hard to imagine losing the love of your life. There's so much I want for my mom. I wish her bones didn't hurt; I wish she had a nice boyfriend; I wish I could buy her a house so she never had to worry about money again.

On Sunday afternoon I finish what little homework I have left and then call Raven. She's not home, so I decide to go to a matinee by myself, leaving my mom doing stretches on the living room floor. I walk down to Tinseltown, this three-storey mall with a theatre, on the edge of Chinatown. Most of the stores inside are empty, and it's got a weird, ghostly feel. Once it was built, the shoppers never came. I guess whoever planned this mall didn't realize the demographics. The theatre is mostly empty, too, which is fine with me. I like seeing movies on my own, but people throw sympathetic looks like I'm a loser for being solo when it's an activity that requires silence anyway.

At school on Monday morning, I arrive determined. I will get good test marks that will mean good grades, which will land me a scholarship so I can go to university, figure out a career, and get a good-paying job. Then I will be able to take care of me and my mother. The government sure wasn't going to do it.

I make it all the way through Earth Science without getting distracted. Then at my locker some girls pass by, snickering. One is Kat, who declares loudly:

"Oh, look. It's Ariel STD."

"Ha ha! ARIEL STD!"

I refuse to let it blow my whole day. In Textiles I finish my halter top, pleased with how it turned out. The teacher likes me, since I'm good at sewing and most of the other kids just fool around. It's nice to hear compliments, and I relish her words of praise. I even decide to wear my new halter top the rest of the day. While walking to French class, Jesse and his friends come by in a noisy horde. My back is to them, when all of a sudden I feel a tickle between my shoulder blades. Someone yanks the halter strap and the top falls down.

"You ASSHOLES!" I shriek, fumbling to pull it up. I'm not wearing a bra, since the Textiles teacher showed me how to put elastic under the cups.

Fat Joey and Mink high-five each other. "Dude, that made my whole day!"

"That made my whole *year!*"

"Sorry," Jesse says. "Can you blame us? You've got the best rack in the school!"

"Assholes," I repeat. Once the straps are knotted securely, I hurry away from the hoots and whistles. I can't focus during my French class and make a ton of grammatical errors. It's bad enough to have Kat and her friends coming down on me, but having Jesse and his buddies act like jerks is too much to take. I stupidly thought we had some kind of friendship.

I search for Raven at noon, but she's not here today. There's no way I can fake my way through a lunch hour. In the afternoon classes I won't be missing much. If Mom is home I'll tell her that, plain and simple. It's a personal day, if you will. But I hope she'll be gone. I don't want explain how unbearable my life feels right now.

I walk far away from school, until I don't see anyone I know. Then I find a spot on a bench in a park and pull an atlas out of my backpack. I find looking at maps very comforting. Already I am planning my escape. Someone passes by me, then stops. I don't even want to look up, but a man's voice says my name:

"Ariel."

"Huh?"

"It's Ariel, right? Ariel with the ice cream." He pushes up his sunglasses, smiling. "It's me, Julian." Today his black hair is slicked back. He's wearing slacks, brogues, and a leather jacket. Everything about him oozes money and confidence.

"Yeah, where's the Cadillac? I remember the fins on it."

"Really?" he says. "I remember *you*. Do you need a ride?"

"Not really," I say.

"You look like a lost Marilyn Monroe."

I stare back down at my atlas, and Julian drops onto the bench beside me. "Going somewhere?"

"Not soon enough."

He leans in closer and I smell soap and cologne. "California? I've driven down the coast a few times to L.A. and back."

"Really?"

"Sure," Julian says. He traces his finger down the coastline on the map. "If you're planning to drive you can make it to San Francisco in a day." I suddenly wonder how old he thinks I am.

"You've got an amazing body," he says low in my ear. "I bet the boys really like you."

I tense and Julian shifts away. "You don't seem very friendly today."

"It's been a rough morning." I'm mortified that I might suddenly burst into tears.

"How could a girl as beautiful as you ever have a bad day?"

"Pssh. I'm not beautiful."

Julian whips out his phone and takes a picture before I can protest. "Just look," he says and shows me the screen.

"Actually, that's not bad," I admit. In the photo my hair hangs over my shoulder and there is a cute look of surprise on my face.

"One more," Julian coaxes, and takes three or four different shots. I start posing and making faces, then I see some kids from school down the block and stand up.

"I should get going."

"Give me your cell number and I'll send these to you."

"Ummm, okay. It's 604-707-3173."

He punches the digits directly in his phone. "Gotcha," he says. The way he says this makes me nervous but excited, too.

It's like he doesn't want to let me go. "Wait," he says, shaking my hand. "Can I give you my card?"

"What for?"

Julian laughs, then opens his wallet and takes out a business card. "Call me anytime. I'd love to shoot you." There must be a strange look on my face because he laughs again and says, "With a camera."

He presses the card into my hand, then leans back on the bench and lights a cigarette. I look down to read what it says:

Julian Taylor, Photographer
Producer/Distributor
Vixen Media, Inc.

* * *

My mom isn't home when I get there. Then I remember that she has physio on Mondays and Thursdays now. She also stops by the magazine office once a week, and usually someone takes her out for lunch. An Aspirin bottle, washcloth, and empty juice container sit on the kitchen counter. Getting older seems to be about new aches and pains, and looking for your glasses. I drop my bag and jacket on the floor, relieved to have the place to myself.

I stash Julian's business card in my dresser, then kick the stuff off my bed and stretch out. Maybe he could take a lot of photos and make me famous. I'd change my name and my hair colour, just like Marilyn Monroe, and move somewhere no one knew me. I look disgustedly through my closet, which is mostly full of thrift store finds and donations from Tish. I own one good coat and two pairs of shoes. Or three, if you count flip-flops. In the mirror I try a variety of poses, then stand for a critical observation; my skin is generally good, and I have pouty lips I colour bright red. There's a small gap between my front teeth I hate. My mom says its good luck. I pile my hair on top of my head and squish my lips at the mirror like they're ready for their close-up.

Pretty soon this gets boring. I make a sandwich and look at some websites, then work on my English essay about the significance of Piggy's glasses in *Lord of the Flies*. What irony, skipping school to do homework. *Pathetic,* I think.

* * *

Over a dinner of stir-fry that night, I tell my mom, "This guy said I looked like Marilyn Monroe today." After physiotherapy, Mom had seen her doctor, and he'd prescribed new pills to add to the pile she took every morning.

"Marilyn Monroe was a tragic character," she says, picking up a baby corn in her chopsticks. "She died at thirty-six of an overdose of booze and sleeping pills." My mom writes a lot about the feminine perspective, and has a book club with some friends from her women's studies class. Once, when I was younger, she took me on a march to protest pay inequality at the university, and I kept loudly pointing out signs that spelled "womyn" wrong.

"Hollywood created Marilyn as a sex symbol, this goddess persona no one is capable of fulfilling," she continues. "Eventually it killed her."

"So, it wasn't a compliment?"

That makes us laugh. Then she picks up the bottle of soy sauce and winces. I notice her hands are swollen. The first finger on her right hand looks almost gnarled. It's alarming that I've never noticed it before.

"It's just the weather changing," she says. "My joints are telling me winter is on the way."

"Maybe there's a cheesy TV movie we can watch tonight."

"Perfect."

So we curl up on either end of the couch in our slippers. Later on I make popcorn, and by some miracle we have both pop and ice cream for floats. When my mom goes to bed, I stay up flicking the channels. It's been such a peaceful day, I've almost forgotten the dread of going back to school.

* * *

"Hey, lady," Raven says, banging my locker door. I haven't seen her at school for a while and she gives me a big bear hug. "How you livin' these days?"

"Could be worse," I say, and it's true. People, namely Kat, have been ignoring me lately, which is a lot better than being harassed. After the strap-pulling incident, Jesse hasn't been around. Now it's just me and the Vietnamese girl. Sometimes she smiles in my direction. Her name is Michelle Phan.

"Are you going to this?" Raven points to a sign for tomorrow's Halloween dance.

"Uh, I don't think so." Events like that bring back memories of sweaty, nervous boys trying to jab inside my mouth with their tongues. During a slow song at my last school dance, some guy got his gum stuck in my hair.

"Good. This guy Sneaky Pete is having a party. Go there instead."

I overheard some kids talking about it, but didn't expect to go. My mom bought candy to give out to kids, but I can't imagine any will come to our street.

"I'm going trick-or-treating with my little cousins," Raven says. "I'll give you the address of the party if you want to meet there later."

"Cool. What's your costume?"

"Anything that doesn't involve trying to be sexy. What about you?"

"I don't know, I was thinking of Marilyn Monroe, but kind of blue in the face."

"Oh, that's good," Raven says.

I know that tomorrow in Textiles we have the class to work on our Halloween costumes. If I get the right kind of material, I could probably make a flowing white skirt. There's a discount fabric store right in the middle of Cracktown, but I hate walking around down there by myself. I already have the halter top, which I have since secured with a row of hooks.

"Any luck finding Albertine?"

"No. I don't know why she's avoiding everyone. I'm gonna run into her sooner or later. And when I do . . ." She smacks her fist on her palm for emphasis.

I have a feeling that Raven doesn't even want to consider that Albertine isn't alive. My thoughts flicker to a news story about the Highway of Tears. It's a stretch of road up north where thirty-two Native women have been murdered or gone missing. The highway runs from Prince George to Prince Rupert, where Albertine lives. Raven said she usually hitchhikes.

"Let's go look for her. Maybe today is the day."

"No," Raven says with dejection. "It probably isn't."

* * *

The party is at a crowded, decrepit house in Strathcona, which is a cluster of once-stately heritage homes now in varying states of disrepair. I stand outside the hedges on Petey's sidewalk smoking a cigarette at the designated meeting time. Finally, I screw up the courage to walk in.

The music is loud bass and pumping hip-hop. There are lots of guys in masks, but some aren't in costume at all, as if they're too cool. I'm relieved to see Raven right away. She's dressed as a killer clown, laughing with some guy in the corner with a skeleton painted on his face.

"Hey, Ariel! Over here."

"Whew," I say. "It's crowded." I'm glad I found her right away.

"Nice outfit," Raven tells me. "At least you put some effort into it. Not like the three sexy kittens or the sexy devil over there." There's a dance party in the living room and a girl in a tight red dress waves a cheap plastic trident. "You got anything to drink?"

"No," I say. I'd spent all my money on making the skirt and buying a pair of cheap white pumps. My mom loved my Marilyn costume idea, and had helped me pin curl my hair and apply the fake eyelashes.

"Ariel, you're on booze patrol."

"Go shake those money-makers," her friend says.

"Shut up, Hutch," Raven warns.

Everyone I pass on the way to the kitchen looks wasted. A couple of guys in ball caps and hoodies stand around the stove. One holds out a burning joint and I take a polite puff.

"What's your name? You're hot," says a guy

dressed like a hobo. Or maybe it's his regular style, it's hard to tell. I say nothing and open the refrigerator.

"Shut up, dumbass! She's obviously not gonna talk to you."

"I love you," the hobo leers.

The fridge is crammed full of cans and bottles. I ask, "Will anyone mind if take one of these beers?"

"What are you willing to do for it?"

The hobo gives me a sloppy smile. "You can if you stay here with me."

"Well, I need one for my friend, too," I say. "But we'll come back and drink them with you." I hurry out of the kitchen and back to Raven. She flicks off the bottle caps with her lighter. It's a cool move.

"Cheers," she says, and we clink bottles. "Five more missions like that and this party might actually seem decent." I snort laughter and a song comes on that I like, so I bust out a few dance moves. It's my hours of practise in front of the TV and all. We finish our beers, and Hutch gives us plastic glasses with rum and watery cola. I shoot mine, and he pours another.

"This is encouraging," he says.

"Shut up, Hutch."

Just then, a bunch of guys stream into the party. It's Jesse, followed by Fat Joey and Mink and a couple more dudes. "Hey, Ariel," Jesse says. "Lookin' good, girl."

I ask, "What are you supposed to be?" He's wearing a flannel shirt and has a bandana around his forehead.

"Myself. That's enough."

"Dude, let's go smoke that joint," his friend says.

Jesse motions at me to come. "I got some killer weed."

"No," I say. "I don't want my top mysteriously falling down like last time."

"Hey, I'm sorry about that," Jesse says, and he actually sounds sincere. And since I've already had a doobie puff, I agree to join them. For some reason, they head into the bathroom. It's a decent size, but we're still pretty cramped.

"Why do we have to squeeze in here?"

"Cuz no one else can handle this loco shit," says this guy dressed as Cheech. Or maybe it's Chong, I forget which.

Right after I take a hit of the joint, I'm stoned. My legs feel kind of weird and numb. The only other time I've smoked weed was when Dina bought a gram from Jamie Fitzpatrick. Tish got so high, she ended up hiding in the closet and we had to coax her out with potato chips.

"That's it for me," I say. "I'm going back to the party."

"No, don't leave. Let's have tub-time!"

I laugh and throw open the door. Two sexy cavewomen lined up for the bathroom eye me suspiciously. On the steps outside, Raven is rolling her eyes at the guy and girl kissing noisily on the sidewalk.

"I puffed a joint in the bathroom," I tell her.

"Now I feel way too stoned."

"I feel like knocking someone out," she answers.

"Ooookay," I say, "on that note, it's time to go home."

We link arms and half-run to the bus stop, cackling like witches.

People love Halloween because it's easy to have courage behind a mask. While waiting on the bus bench, some old guy in a Subaru cruises the block twice, asking how much I cost.

Chapter 6

On Monday morning I'm late for school and rush down the hallway, shaking my wet hair from the rain. I don't even notice until I get to my locker, and there it is, spray-painted right on the door:
SKANK
The letters are thick and black, dripping. My instinct is to walk right past the locker like it isn't mine. But then I notice a few kids whispering and looking at me, even the nice ones. Even Michelle Phan.

My shaking hands spin the combination lock. I put my backpack inside and take out my French book and *Lord of the Flies*. But instead of class I go straight to the office. The secretary comes to the counter and I tell her, "My locker has been vandalized." She peers over her glasses at me with pursed lips like somehow this is my fault.

"Locker number?'

"363."

"Name?'

"Ariel Stark."

"All right Ariel. Go to class and I'll call maintenance. The principal may wish to speak with you."

In the middle of French, as I'm trying to understand past participles, the intercom crackles. "Ariel Stark, come to the office please."

I don't get up fast enough and the teacher, Mrs. Dupois, barks at me. "*Allez-toi!*"

"I'm going," I mutter.

"*En FRANCAIS!*"

My mind becomes blank. All the French I have ever learned has somehow magically been erased from my brain. The silence gets longer and the kids start to snicker. "*Je comprende*," I say lamely, and hurry out of class.

I wait on the hard plastic chairs outside of the principal's office with two Native boys dressed in baggy pants and jerseys. No one says anything. Then they get called in to see the vice principal. He's the one that hands out punishments. Word is he's an ex-army sergeant. If you get sent to see him, it means trouble. There are 750 people at my school, and lots of fights. People get suspended all the time.

The principal opens his office door. "Ariel, come in." He's a tall, skinny man with a bald head and glasses, wearing a wrinkled grey suit.

He looks down at a paper on his desk. "Your locker is being repainted."

"Okay."

"Are you having problems in school, Ariel?"

"My grades are good," I reply, but I have a sinking feeling where this is going.

"Why would someone deface your locker in this manner?"

"I have no idea."

"And am I to assume you possess not one idea who might have done it?"

"No, I don't."

Then the phone buzzes and he answers. After a moment, he excuses himself and leaves the room. I sit and stare at the walls until the principal returns. After settling back into the leather chair behind his desk, he clears his throat. "Well, we'll try to find who's responsible. Your new locker assignment is 217."

Oh great, I think. The two hundred lockers are down in the section for eighth graders. Is there a location where I could possibly look more out of place?

"And Ariel, I'd like you to see a counsellor."

"What for?"

"It's been brought to my attention there was a certain incident a few weeks ago involving you and a group of boys in the hallway."

"I don't know what you're talking about," I falter.

"We are looking into it nonetheless." The principal leans back in his chair and looks at me for a long, uncomfortable minute. "You're excused," he says.

* * *

The rumour of the week is that I gave a bunch of guys a blowjob in the bathroom of the party. I know this because Raven tells me. When people point in the hallway and whisper at me, it's not paranoia. Anyone could have made this story up, and it doesn't matter what's true or not. Everyone loves a good piece of gossip. And it's not like any of the guys are rushing to set the record straight.

Vancouver can be a very difficult place to live because of the endless cold rain. And the weather lately only adds to my depression. Occasionally, in the winter it snows, and then we might at least get some sunshine. But mostly the sky is grey, the cement is grey, and the mountains begin to feel like they're closing in. The worst part of winter this year is how it affects my mom. Her arthritis becomes aggravated; and it hurts to move her ankles, knees, and especially her hips. All her joints get red and swollen. The doctors have raised her doses of medication, but it doesn't seem to be helping.

I notice how badly she is limping at the grocery store. She is using her cane, and there are little wet patches on the grimy store linoleum that keep causing her to slip.

"Get in the cart," I say. "I'll push you."

It makes her laugh. "Cantaloupe or honeydew?" she asks. "You need to eat more fruit."

"I like strawberries," I say, picking up a package.

"They're not in season. Oh my, these are terribly expensive . . ."

And then I see her. Katrina Kubalowski. She's

on the other side of the produce section, staring at me with an evil smile. Her bleached skunk-stripes are now bright pink and match her lipstick. My hands get sweaty and my heart starts pounding. I'm scared Kat is going to make a scene in front of my mom. I swing my cart around so my back is to her.

"Jeez mom, can you stop feeling up the melons, please? I'd like to get out of here sometime tonight."

My mom shakes her head and puts some bananas in the cart. "Teenage hormones," she says wearily to the woman next to her. They share sympathetic looks.

"Mom," I hiss, "you're embarrassing me. I can't stand grocery shopping with you."

"Shush," she tells me, weighing a bag of oranges.

We used to have a Volvo, but it died a few years ago, and my mom didn't have the money to fix it or get another car. Either we have to take a cab home or lug all these groceries on the bus. I pray she has money left over for a taxi. We do a big grocery run once a month when she gets her disability cheque, and it's always an excruciating event.

My mom goes up and down every aisle, even the one with pet supplies. She checks and rechecks prices, and reads all the labels. The whole time I'm terrified that Kat is going to jump out from behind a display like some horrible teenage ninja. I start to relax when we push the cart into the checkout aisle. Maybe she just ran in to buy a bag of chips or something. I might have gotten lucky.

"And I have a coupon for the laundry soap," my mom tells the cashier, a frazzled-looking woman with tattoos.

"You have coupons?" I say with disbelief.

"Shush," my mom says again. "And the oatmeal was on sale as well."

After an eternity, the groceries are bagged and I call for a taxi. "*See*, Mom? Cell phones come in pretty handy," I crow. The metal doors slide open, and I push the cart outside into the cool night air. My mom limps beside me.

"Smart ass," she laughs, and playfully swats me.

Someone says, "Yeah, kick her ass."

It's Kat, standing right by the front doors. Her friend laughs, some girl with plucked-away eyebrows and heavy eyeliner. I start pushing the cart faster. "I'm glad it isn't raining tonight," I say to Mom to distract her. "Let's just hail a cab, it'll be faster. I think one's coming."

"Sweetie, slow down a bit," she puffs.

"TAXI," I holler.

It stops and I start throwing bags in the trunk. I hear laughter and don't want to turn around to look, but I do. Kat is walking stiff-legged like my mom, only more exaggerated like a hunchback. Her friend makes a bunch of stupid sounds and says, "What is she, a retard or something?"

If my mom hears or notices, she doesn't let on. We finish loading the groceries and as the taxi drives us home, I see the inside. I think how satisfying it would have been to run across the parking lot and smash Katrina Kubalowski in the face. My mom starts talking about dinner. "Let's do something simple," she says. "Maybe soup and grilled cheese sandwiches. How about a nice salad, too?"

"Sure, Mom," I say. "That sounds good." But I'm completely oblivious to anything but thoughts of revenge.

I've *had* it.

Chapter 7

The next day is Friday, and it's a Professional Development Day for the teachers, so we don't have to go. My mom lies on the couch, alternating between curled up with a hot water bottle and a novel, and TV channels and ice packs. Nothing seems to comfort her. I decide to get out of the house so she can have some quiet.

I call Raven, but no one picks up. Then I try Dina, who answers in her excited, breathless way.

"Hi, Ariel!"

"Hey, what are doing today?"

"I'm at Metrotown with Tish. We're about to see a movie."

"Which one?"

She names a 3D movie that just opened. "I wanted to see that."

"Our friend Cassandra drove. But come and meet us after."

Metrotown is a gigantic shopping centre with an arcade and movie complex. The Skytrain goes right there, but it's a long train ride, and usually filled with preteen wannabe gangsters and other vicious little posses.

"I'm broke," I say.

"Just look around then."

"It's never as much fun if you know you can't buy anything. I guess I'll stick around here today."

"In your '*hood?* Have fun with that. I'll see you at Tish's for the sleepover."

"That's not for a couple of weeks." We chat a bit longer and hang up.

My mom is snoring on the couch, and I decide to walk down to a coffee shop. Maybe I'll see Raven out and about somewhere. I leave a note and close the door carefully behind me.

Outside, the streets are spotted with puddles. The air feels like the rain is on hold but could start again at any minute. I walk along, swinging my umbrella. It's good to have if it starts raining and equally good if you have to jab someone in the eye. I pass three people sleeping on cardboard under an awning. Their heads are covered with blankets, and it looks like they're dead. Wet garbage clings to the gutters, and a woman walks by me barefoot, in a daze. Her head has been shaved. Raven told me dealers do this to mark women who owe drug debts. It lets everybody know.

I tuck my chin into my collar and keep going, ignoring the occasional whistle or catcall. "Nice bucket," I hear.

"Nice caboose!"

I speed-walk all the way down past the porno shops and Pigeon Park and soup kitchens when a display in a store window catches my eye. It's a place called Modele that I've passed many times before. The mannequins wear lingerie and see-through dresses. On a whim, I walk in.

There's a whole section of thigh-high boots and spiked heels, another section of latex body wear. It's some kind of fetish store, and I wish Raven was here so we could have a laugh. There's a rack of sale dresses in the back I look through, and I pull out a silky mini-dress with a scooped neck. The price tag says $149.99, but I hold it up to myself in the mirror anyway. It's far beyond the twenty bucks in my pocket.

Then I hear voices at the register. I turn and see that it's Julian, with a voluptuous redhead in skimpy clothes. My instinct is to duck behind the rack and hide. I peek out and watch as he pays for some lingerie. The redhead rubs against him and coos. I wonder who this woman is and how she knows Julian. He slaps her ass and she makes an "ooooh" sound. Then they leave together.

"Beautiful, beautiful," says the salesman coming toward me. The man is short and squat, and there's black chest hair sticking out of his shirt collar. His thick accent sounds Russian or something. "You try on."

I put the hanger back, embarrassed. "It's too much for me," I say. "No money today."

"You try on," he repeats, taking the dress off the rack. My refusals fall on deaf ears. "Then put on shoes for me." He's staring at my ratty sneakers.

I blurt out, "Only if you give me that dress." I'm surprised when he nods in agreement.

"Yes, yes. We make exchange." My brain tries to formulate a reason why this is wrong but can't think of one. Besides, it's a beautiful dress.

In the tiny change room I take a quick look around for hidden cameras, then yank off my shoes, jeans, and sweater. The dress is short and tight in all the right places. The elastic under the boobs pushes them up somewhere around my collar bone. I pull back the curtain and walk out in bare feet.

"Now put on shoes and walk." The salesman leads me to the shoe section and points to a chair. Then he comes back with a pair of spike heels in my size, slips them on my feet. I wobble as I stand, then go up and down the aisles dutifully.

"Beautiful," he says again, motioning for me to sit down. He kneels and pulls off a shoe. Then to my surprise and horror, he holds it to his nose and takes a deep sniff. I race back to the change room and quickly change clothes. When I come out, the salesman is still cradling the shoe.

"Your name?" he asks.

"Katrina," I call over my shoulder. I shove the dress in my bag and burst out the door, back to the anonymous street.

It could be a funny story, but I'm not sure who to tell.

Monday morning I wake up and put on the dress with a pair of leggings and a throw a cardigan on overtop. But as soon as I get to school, I take these off in the bathroom and put on a pair of fishnets and my ankle boots. The dress really shows off my curves. All year I've been wearing hoodies and baggy clothes to hide them, but not today. As I walk down the hall, I hear one of the eighth grade boys say, "How *old* is Ariel?"

"I don't know," another answers. "I think twenty-five!"

A couple of guys do a double take as I walk by, and their reaction makes me smile. I drop into my seat in Earth Science with flair. Everyone is looking at me, and this time it's not for being the butt of a joke. Even Tae Won, the brain of the class, glances over, so I beam at him. He quickly looks back down at his book with a look of pure terror.

The girl in front of me is twisted all the way around in her seat. She's got a freckled face wrinkled in disdain.

"What?" I snap. "Mind your own business and turn around."

I'm a solid girl, and tough to take down. She whips herself around to face the front. Then the teacher walks in and opens his briefcase. Class begins.

* * *

76

I like Mondays because it's a day when Raven usually comes to school. But after this semester she'll have enough credits to graduate, so I'll have to get used to not seeing her here anymore.

We meet at this donair place where everyone goes. She's in a booth, and her eyes get big when she sees me. "Where'd you get that *dress?*"

"Modele."

"You went to the hooker store? That's hilarious," Raven says. "What's the deal? You're so dressed up today."

"Nothing's up," I say. "If I want to wear this dress, I'll wear it. I'm sick of worrying I'll offend people who already hate me for stupid reasons." Then I see Jesse and Mink push their way into the line. "Hold on a second. Hey Jesse," I call, walking over.

"Ari-*el*. That's a hot dress."

"You like it? Thanks," I flirt, touching his elbow. "I miss seeing you at my locker."

"Yeah, where'd you go?"

"I got reassigned. Some children like to finger-paint," I say loudly. "Besides, I didn't see you at school for awhile."

"Yeah, I kind of got kicked out of my house," Jesse says, grinning. He really is cute, with his ball cap turned backwards and skateboard under his arm.

"Where do you live then?"

"I just skate every night with Mink and then crash on an air mattress on his floor."

I squeeze beside him in line, so we're pressed

against each other. "I don't have any money for lunch today," I pout. "Does being homeless mean you won't buy me any fries?"

"Sure I will," he says. "But what are you gonna do for me?"

I give Jesse a little shrug and wink. "Name your price." Mink's eyeballs are about ready to pop out of his head.

"Oh, I'll think of something."

"Thank you sooo much," I say sweetly when he orders my fries. "You're a doll." Then I give him a big hug.

When I get back to the table with the fries, Raven gives me a look. "What was THAT about?"

I whisper, "Oh my god, I can't believe that worked!"

"That guy has a brain the size of a walnut," Raven says. "And you're surprised that all it took was a little flirting to get some food out of him?"

I've already told her about the incident in the parking lot of the grocery store. "Katrina Kubalowski is my enemy," I remind her. "And anything that pisses her off is fine with me."

"That's dangerous," she warns.

I'm kind of annoyed that I'm not getting more support for not being a doormat. I push the paper plate toward her. "Have a fry," I say. We eat silently, watching people come in and out, neither one of us saying a word.

Chapter 8

Finally winter break starts, and I have three glorious weeks of no school.

My mom takes me shopping down the long row of shops on Granville Street. Or rather, I take her. She's using a walker that her physiotherapist recommended, and I grip her arm to make sure she doesn't slip on the icy sidewalk. Shoppers loaded down with parcels barrel past, while small pockets of Christmas carols assault our ears. A woman pushing a stroller narrowly misses us.

"I hate those me-first mommies," I say.

"Well, *someone's* not feeling the Christmas spirit," my mom says.

I'm not being festive at all. I haven't seen Raven since the semester ended, and now she's up in Prince Rupert for Christmas. Some relative was giving her and her aunties a ride. I really don't want

Raven to dislike me. When you've only got three friends in the world, you hang onto them tight.

Right now I'm shopping for Dina and Tish. Our annual sleepover and gift exchange is coming up at Tish's place. I've already taken care of my mom. I made her a fuzzy cover for her hot water bottle, and bought a cookbook she's been wanting. My mom is easy to shop for. She likes everything. Dina and Tish, on the other hand, are the exact opposite and have picky tastes. We walk into a clothing store with big sale signs. High-speed Christmas jingles blast as I look through the accessories.

"I can't afford anything," I grumble.

"You can always look for a job," my mom says.

"Yeah, but you know I hate work."

This makes us laugh. Finally I decide on a leopard print scarf and hoop earrings for Dina, and a pair of mittens embroidered with owls for Tish. "Let's go sit down somewhere," my mom says. "How about a hot chocolate?"

On the way to the till I see a leather jacket on display that I have to try on. It's got the right amount of snaps and buckles, with a red satin lining. The jacket is a perfect fit when I check out my reflection in the mirror. I look tough.

My mom sits on the padded seat of the walker, waiting. When she sees the jacket on me, she claps in approval. "It looks great, honey."

"I LOVE this jacket. This is all I want for Christmas for the rest of my life."

She lifts up the price tag. "Ariel, it costs $300!

That's almost half our rent for the month."

"I'll throw in all the money I've got, too."

My mom shakes her head. "I'm sorry, sweetie. It's just not realistic."

"Excuse me," I say, stopping a salesgirl in a Santa hat. "Is this jacket part of your sale, too?"

"Noooo," she answers. "Just the stuff on the front rack."

"Will it go on sale anytime soon?" I'm starting to sound desperate.

"I don't think so. Soooo-rry." But the clerk doesn't sound very genuine. She looks me up and down then flounces away.

I slip off the leather jacket with dejection. "It's just a coat," my mom says. But there's more to it than that. It made me feel like someone not to be messed with. And I need all the armour I can get.

* * *

The night of Tish's sleepover my mom is going out for dinner with a friend, and they give me a ride to Kits. We drive right past our old street on the way, but my mom and I don't mention it.

Tish lives in a gigantic house with a stone fence and shrubs around the property. Her parents separated last year but her dad came back a few months later. He's still forced to stay in one of the guestrooms. I've seen Mr. Walker very little over the years, and we like to joke that Tish's mom keeps him wrapped in plastic in the living room no one is

81

allowed to enter. Not only is her mother is a religious freak, she is also obsessed with germs. It's kind of tiring to hang out at Tish's house because of it. We usually have the sleepover at Dina's, but this year her parents went on a Mediterranean cruise. Her grandmother is staying there and Dina isn't allowed visitors.

I ring the bell and hear Tish bellow, "I've GOT it!" She opens the door and squeals. "You're here!"

"Tushy," I smile, using our old nickname.

"A-Bomb!" We give each other an affectionate hug.

I notice Tish's mother standing at the top of the staircase, looking down. "Hello, Mrs. Walker."

"Hello, Ariel." There is a can of aerosol spray ready in her hand.

"Shoes off," Tish whispers.

I slip them onto the designated spot and follow Tish to the giant den. Behind me Mrs. Walker comes down the hall and wipes the wall where I was standing. It's something that would offend most people, but I'm used to it. Their bathrooms are as sterile as an operating room.

The den has wood-panelling and there's a crackling fire. Dina is curled on one of the big comfy couches, laughing with a girl beside her I don't know.

"Ariel, baby!"

"Hey, Dina."

"This is Cassandra."

I drop my pillow and sleeping bag on the floor.

"Hi, Cassandra." I wave. She's got short black hair and perfect white teeth, and sits cross-legged in Juicy Couture sweatpants and slipper Uggs.

"Hi," she says.

"Do people ever call you Cassie?" I ask.

"It's Cah-*sondra*."

Tish's mom brings in a cracker tray with pickles and cheeses and chips and chocolate squares. This is followed by paper plates, cutlery, and a giant stack of napkins. "Don't worry if you spill on the floor," she trills, but there's an anxious look on her face.

"Get lost, Mother," Tish tells her. Even though she's supposed to be Christian, Tish is always pretty rude to her mom.

We immediately attack the food tray. "Oh my god," Dina says with her mouth full of dip, "Ariel, have your boobs gotten even *bigger?*"

"I hope not," I say. "But you're not exactly one to talk." Dina is short and curvaceous and chubby, which she blames on being Greek. Her house is always filled with baking trays of golden spanako-pita or honey-soaked baklava.

Cassandra asks, "How do you guys know each other?"

"We went to school together. My house used to be just down the street."

"I *heard* about you," Cassandra says, in way I can't decide is friendly or not. She lists the classes she has with Dina and Tish, and for a while they talk about people I don't know.

"Dina, do you ever see Rory anymore?" I ask

when the conversation breaks.

"Ohhh, grossies! I'm so over that guy."

"Now she loves Finn."

"Who's Finn?"

"Finnegan," Dina says dreamily. "Oh my god, he's so cute." I follow the conversation for a full five minutes until I realize she's talking about some guy on a TV show.

"I'm pretty sure he's gay," I tell her.

"Nuh-uh, Miss Thang," Cassandra snaps her fingers at me. "No he's NOT."

"I don't care," Dina says. "He can be my gay boyfriend."

After we finish with the snack tray and Mrs. Walker secures the perimeter with her hand-held vacuum, the girls decide it's time for the gift exchange. My mom bought the cheap wrapping paper, the kind that easily tears. The side of Tish's package has split and bulges obscenely.

Cassandra giggles. "Nice gift-wrapping."

Tish holds up her mittens. "I love these. They're cute."

"I know you're into owls."

"I'm not *into* them."

Dina opens her present and winds the scarf around her neck. From her smile when she thanks me, I can tell it's the right gift. "Okay, now you and Cassandra get yours."

We both receive a basket full of oils and bath salts from Lush. Then Cassandra passes out two small boxes wrapped with red foil and taped with a sparkly bow. Dina and Tish open the lids, gasping. Both girls hold up thick silver bracelets.

"OOOOoo, it's gorgeous! It must have cost *a lot*."

"Look, they're engraved!"

"D-T-C. Dina, Tish, Cassandra."

"And the date!"

"Is this real silver?"

"This is my favourite gift ever!"

It's an awkward moment but no one notices but me. For a while we sit around and talk about boys and bands we like. Then Tish puts a movie on her large screen TV. It's some horrible romantic comedy, and we end up talking over it.

"So, Ariel, are there any cute guys in your school?"

"Some," I say. "But they're high school boys. I flirt with this one guy, Jesse, but that's about it. It's pretty boring."

"Just watch out that he doesn't turn into another Patrick."

"Who's that?" Cassandra asks.

"That's Ariel's ex-boyfriend. She totally had sex with him," Tish says matter-of-factly.

"Tish, do you mind?"

"Ariel *always* has a boyfriend," Dina adds.

Patrick and I had gone out for over a year, which is another reason it was good to change schools. He wanted to spend all his time with me, and things got too intense. There were constant phone calls and he'd post messages to me hourly. Patrick didn't take it well when I broke up with him. He punched a car window at a party, and once he saw me at the movies and broke the display case where they put the movie posters and his arm got all bloody. It caused a lot of drama, and his friends hated me because I refused to take him back.

"I don't think Ariel's been single since third grade!"

"Slut," Cassandra says, and they giggle.

"Let's put our jammies on." Tish yawns. "We still have a scary movie to watch."

I feel self-conscious and go to the bathroom to change. The movie is already playing when I come out. On an air mattress on the floor are Dina, Tish, and Cassandra, lying side by side on their stomachs. I stretch my sleeping bag on the couch. It's the first time since fifth grade that anyone else has been at our slumber party. The movie is a remake of some old movie and there's lots of gore and bad acting. Even a house cat jumps out to scare someone. When this happens, Cassandra screams and the girls laugh, but she's the loudest, practically hysterical.

"Don't die laughing," I say. No one says anything. I roll over and shut my eyes.

* * *

In the morning their chatter wakes me up. "You *snore*," Cassandra says, before I even have a chance to say good morning.

"Breakfast," we hear Tish's mom call from upstairs.

"We're COMING," Tish bellows. "Tired," she

says, rolling over on her pillow. Then she rolls back over again. "I'm *hungry*."

I go to the bathroom with my pile of clothes and overnight bag. After washing my face, I start to get dressed and my bra is missing. I check my bag but it's not there, so I pull on my sweatshirt and search around the couch.

"I can't find my bra," I say. Everyone titters.

"You fell asleep first," Cassandra says. "Fair game at a slumber party."

"Where the hell is it?"

"Sorry," Tish says, and gets up. She comes back with a frozen plank of brassiere. "We put it in the freezer."

"WHAT?"

"Its fair game at a slumber party," Dina repeats.

"Well hardy-har. Thanks a lot."

It's the kind of thing we've done to each other on and off through the years, like shaving cream in the hand, a felt pen mustache. I try to laugh it off, but then Cassandra grabs my bra and yells, "It's humongous! I could paddle a raft with this thing."

"BREAKFAST!" we hear again. I cross my arms and follow the girls upstairs. There's something in the way they continue to cackle that gives me a familiar sinking feeling.

* * *

Mr. Walker drops me off at home in his Escalade. Pulling up, he looks at my house dubiously. "Are you

87

going to be okay?" he asks. "Should I walk you in?"

I clutch my pillow and sleeping bag and Lush basket, fumbling for my keys. "I'm fine. Thanks, Mr. Walker." The last thing I want is him coming to the door.

Inside my house it's warm and smells like nutmeg and cinnamon. My mom is in the kitchen pulling out a batch of sugar cookies.

"Mmmmmm, those look good."

"How was the sleepover?"

"It was alright."

"And Dina and Tish? How are the girls?"

"Hmm, let's see. Tish is getting an iPad for Christmas and Dina's parents are on their second cruise this year. They've already been to Alaska."

"Lovely," my mom says. She looks over and sees the sour expression on my face. "What's wrong, sweetheart?"

"Nothing," I shrug. "It's just that they've got a new friend now. Her name's Cassandra."

"Is she nice?"

"I don't know. Not really. It just feels like she's taken my place."

My mom begins to take the cookies off the sheet and slip them onto cooling racks. "Well, it was bound to happen. You girls don't see each other very often, especially going to different schools. It's natural that you grew apart."

"It sucks," I say.

"Have a cookie," my mom says.

Chapter 9

The best thing about Christmas is that a few days before, Uncle Jack will come to town. Every year he's like our own personal Santa Claus and brings us a bag of presents. My mom even buys a free-range turkey, an occasion that happens only once a year. She says I can eat meat if I want, but I have to cook it myself, so I never bother. We also make eggnog, and last year I even got some with a bit of rum.

The day of his visit, my mom gets me up early to start the turkey. I stuff it for her, too, so as not to traumatize the vegetarian. Then we wash the floors, scrub the bathroom, take out the garbage. Afterwards my mom lies down to have a nap. I squirt the turkey with juice every so often, and decide to get the potatoes chopped and ready to make it easier for my mom. I know this time of year is hard on her. She really misses my dad. I can tell because after a few cups of eggnog, she pulls out the photo albums. On Christmas Day we are always invited to one of her friends' houses, but it's not the same when you're trying to join a stranger's family, staring at someone's tree and talking to people you don't really know.

As I stand at the counter peeling potatoes, my thoughts drift to my dad. All I have left of him are the fragments of memory I can still conjure up: the tickle of his mustache when he kissed me. The way he smelled like wood smoke and cigarettes. How his hands were so big I just held on to one finger as I crossed the street. For years I pretended he was just out on the road, and any day he would walk through the door again.

My dad was the soundman for a huge eighties rock band. My parents met when my mom interviewed the group for the magazine. She sat at the soundboard during the show, and my dad convinced her to ride to the next gig with him. The story is that she stayed on the bus all the way to Boston. They got married six months later. It's quite a romantic tale, until my dad died when I was six. He was killed when one of the tour buses slid down an embankment and rolled. Everyone survived but him. I'd read on the Internet how my dad was found under the bus with his legs sticking out. Some people had left comments and thought that was funny. Stuff like that used to bother me, but what hurts now are all the things that will never happen, like having a father to walk me down the aisle at my wedding. My future kids will have one grandfather less. Maybe they won't have one at all.

It's weird to think how the slightest change in direction can affect your life forever.

* * *

"Uncle Jack!" I yell gleefully, throwing open the door. There's a heavy rain outside and he looks soaked to the bone just getting from the car to the house. "Come on in."

He shakes off his coat and kisses me on the forehead. "You get more beautiful every time I see you," he says.

"Don't tell her that," my mom comes in smiling. "She'll get a big ego."

"That face should be in movies. It'll be famous one day."

"I already am," I say. "Notorious."

They laugh at that and then Mom asks, "Where's Cathy?"

"She's at the hotel. She's not feeling well." But Uncle Jack pauses too long before adding, "I think it's a migraine." It kind of sounds like he's lying.

"She didn't come for dinner last year either," I say. "It was something about —"

"Gastrointestinal problems," my mom finishes.

"Well, she sends her love. That cooking bird smells great!"

The turkey is crispy brown on the outside, and the meat is cooked to perfection. We sit down to bowls of mashed potatoes, cranberries, stuffing, yams baked with marshmallow topping, and boats of gravy. Uncle Jack tries to pass me the Brussels sprouts.

"No, thanks," I say.

"Who is this kid that doesn't like Brussels sprouts?"

"They look like little brains." Uncle Jack laughs and shakes his head. I notice he's wearing a tie this year.

After dessert of apple pie and whipped cream, we sit and hold our bellies. My mom finishes her glass of wine then abruptly remarks, "This spring it will be ten years that Mitch has been gone." I know she's tipsy because she never brings up my dad like that sober.

"It's hard to believe it's been that long."

"Not for me, Jack," she says. "I think about him every day."

"We all miss him." Uncle Jack reaches over and grabs my mom's hand. I feel panicky, like it's going to get all heavy and emotional. It's the perfect time to start scraping dishes into the garbage. I fill the sink with soapy water and plunge my hands in. Christmas can be a brutal time with all those nostalgic ads of perfect families: mommy, daddy, happy kids, and a heap of presents. They don't have commercials for a single mom and her dead husband's best friend and a teenage kid.

"Remember our trip to Spain?" my mom reminisces. "That week at the farm house outside Valencia . . ."

". . . in the middle of an orange grove. Mitch wore a pair of Speedos the whole time, it was so hot."

"Cathy and I went to the most amazing flea market," my mom says. "Ariel, you would have loved it. That's where I got the hallway rug. Oh, and what about that night in Barcelona? We must have drank three bottles of red wine each. I remember walking back to the hotel at dawn."

"The streets were still full of people."

"Catalonia," my mom says, sounding wistful.

I've heard all the tour stories before. My parents travelled all over the world together before I came along. Uncle Jack used to run the merchandise for the band, which was a huge operation. My mom and Aunt Cathy flew out on tours across Europe and America, even Japan. I always got the feeling my mom was kind of a wild chick back in the day. But it sounds like a great life, and she wrote stories for the magazine from the road. Her and my dad would rent a car and follow the bus around. Everyone in the band adored her. When he was killed, they gave my mom a bunch of money and paid for a big funeral. I remember a man playing mournful bagpipes as we stood around the gravesite. There were photographers there snapping pictures of the band members. Everyone stared at me, patted my head and tried to hug me, but I just held onto my mom's hand and cried. For a while the band stayed in contact with my mom, and she'd go to their concerts when they were in town. But I don't think she's heard from them in years. The only one who didn't forget about us is Uncle Jack.

The dishes are done, and I pull the plug and turn around. Uncle Jack's hand is covering my mom's. They are looking into each other's eyes in a way that goes on too long. I begin to wipe the table, and my mom pulls her hand away.

"Let's see you open your presents," Uncle Jack says. "It's close enough to Christmas, isn't it?"

We gather in the living room. My mom opens a card that contains a gift certificate to a department store and another for a supermarket. "Well, thank you, Jack. We can definitely use these. You wouldn't believe how much food a teenager goes through in a week."

"She's still a growing girl."

"Let's hope not," I say, peeling the wrapping paper off a box. My gift is a shiny red iPod, with a docking station and everything. "Oh my god, this is awesome!"

"You spoil her," my mom says.

"Thank you, Uncle Jack," I say and give him a hug. Then my mom hugs him, too, and I can't tell if I'm being paranoid or if something is going on between them. "Don't forget to thank Aunt Cathy," I say loudly.

Afterwards we sit down at the table and play Rummoli. I try to focus on the game, but all night long I can't shake the feeling I've seen something I shouldn't.

* * *

New Year's Eve comes with little excitement. Dina and Tish go skiing in Whistler with Cassandra, whose parents rented a chalet. Raven still isn't back from Prince Rupert, and my mom doesn't feel well, so we watch the ball drop on TV and then go to bed. A few days later, I turn seventeen. What sucks about having your birthday the first week of January is that no one is ever around, or they're broke from the holidays, or caught some flu bug. I celebrate by eating my free lunch at Denny's with my mom and seeing a matinee at Tinseltown. When the movie is over, she lets me spend her Christmas gift card at the department store on clothes. After dinner at a sushi restaurant we go home and I blow out the candles on my homemade birthday cake, all seventeen.

It's been raining steadily since the dinner with Uncle Jack, and my mom is moving around even more stiffly, always rubbing her left hip. The day after my birthday, she comes into the living room where I'm reading a book, and sits down on the couch.

"Sweetie, I have to tell you something." I feel nervous, especially when she says, "I didn't want to ruin Christmas or your birthday."

"What is it, Mom?"

"The hospital called, and I'm booked for hip surgery in two weeks."

"What? You should have told me. I mean, are things that bad?"

She explains how her hip joint has eroded and

the surgeon will replace it with a plastic and metal implant cemented into place. After the surgery she'll need weeks of physiotherapy in a rehabilitation hospital.

"But after all that, the doctor says I should be able to walk without any pain. Isn't that great news?"

"Yeah," I say worriedly. "It's just, you know, pretty major."

"I talked to Uncle Jack, but he and Cathy are busy with work and won't be able to stay here."

"Mom, I just turned seventeen!" I protest. "I can stay by myself."

"It's three weeks, Ariel. Are you sure?"

"I'll come and visit you every day. You're going to be okay though, right?"

"Sure," she smiles. But when I lean over to give her a hug I feel her bones through her sweater, how frail she has become.

* * *

The morning of the surgery, my mom wakes me up to say goodbye. "I'm going now," she says. "The hospital will call later and let you know everything is fine." I squeeze my arms around her neck and feel like crying.

My mom pats my back reassuringly. "Sweetie, the taxi's waiting." I decide that today I should not have to go to school, and turn off my alarm before falling back asleep. The ringing telephone wakes me up around noon.

"Hello?"

"Ariel Stark? This is Vancouver General Hospital. Your mom is out of surgery and in the recovery room doing just fine."

"Thanks for calling," I say, relieved. "When are visiting hours?"

"She's heavily sedated right now. It's best to come tomorrow after dinner."

The next morning I have to force myself to get dressed and go to school. All my least favourite subjects are this term, including the dreaded Algebra class. I snap my locker shut and walk past the rows of grade eight boys.

"Bouncy, bouncy," one says. They sound like donkeys when they laugh. The years between me and these kids seem like dog years. I get to my Biology lab and sit at the first table in the front row. My partner is a smart, chubby kid and every time he looks at me, the tips of his ears turn bright red.

"Look," someone says. "Neville's getting a boner!" My lab partner sneaks a sideways glance and his face reddens.

"Someone get a microscope," I say. The hooting gets even louder. I know it's mean, but at least they're not laughing at me.

After school I walk down to Oppenheimer Park to meet Raven. She's back from Prince Rupert, and says she missed me. It's not raining anymore but the benches are still wet. The grass is covered in pigeons, heads bobbing in their jerky walk, looking for seeds. A crow squawks in a tree like it's pissed off at me for something. And then I see Raven stalking across the park with a thunderous look.

"What's wrong?" I ask with alarm.

She plops down beside me on the bench. "Oh, I just wasted my whole day waiting for my mom because she's a fucking junkie. She's gotten worse since Albertine went missing. That's how she deals with it."

"My mom had her hip surgery yesterday."

"How is she?"

"Good, I guess. I'm going to visit after dinner." The burden of worrying about my mom's health weighs down on me. Sometimes it's a lot of stress and I think, *but I'm only seventeen.*

"Call me after," Raven says.

After heating up a can of soup for dinner, I take two buses to the hospital. I feel bad that I'm bare-handed, but I know Mom will get mad if I spend grocery money to bring her flowers. At the information desk I get her room number and take the elevator to the seventh floor. The door is closed and there's a giant bouquet beside her bed.

"Hey, Mom," I say softly. She's hooked up to an IV. There are tubes sticking out of her neck and her arm, and more coming out from under the blankets. Her skin is so pale I can see the blue veins through the skin.

"Ooooh, hi honey," she croaks, opening her eyes. "I sure feel funny."

"You sound like you got some good painkillers," I say, trying to joke. "How about giving me some?"

My mom groans and pushes the pain button.

"Did you see your flowers?" I read the card to her. "Best Wishes, Cathy and Jack."

"She's not mad at me anymore," she mumbles.

"Who? Aunt Cathy?"

"Mmmmhhh."

"Why would she be mad at you?" But my mom's eyes droop shut and she dozes off again.

I put my jacket on and walk outside. In the smoking area I bum a cigarette off some guy who lights it for me and then I flip open my phone to call Raven.

When she answers I say, "Let's find a party tonight."

Chapter 10

Raven and I walk down to The Plaza, this skate spot underneath an overpass. We watch Jesse and some of his friends skate for a while. There's an older guy there on a board and some kids are laughing. "It's like watching my dad," one of them says.

Then I see Jesse and he cruises over. "What's up, hos?"

"Don't call us that," Raven says, "or I'll knock your block off."

Jesse laughs and does a kick flip, landing on his board. He does another and misses.

"Ha ha," Raven says.

"Is there anything going on tonight?" I pull a cooler out of my bag and crack it open. It only took ten minutes of asking in front of the liquor store before some guy agreed to go in and buy them for me.

"Gimme some of that bitch-pop," Jesse says, and I hand it over. Raven rolls her eyes at me and

I know she can't figure out why I find such an obnoxious boy amusing. I can't really explain it myself.

"Don't drink it all," Raven tells him.

"There's some party later," he says, handing the bottle back to me. I pull my lip gloss out of my bag.

"Is it cool if we show up?"

"Whatever," Jesse shrugs. "Or don't be all business. Just hang here. Check this out," he says, then pushes off to grind across a rail.

Raven and I get comfortable and sip our coolers. Tonight I want to get out of my head, and not have to think about my mom lying in that hospital bed, or about her and Uncle Jack. Raven grabs someone's board and takes it for a ride. She glides effortlessly, drops into the bowl as the guys stand around watching. I can't believe someone this cool is a friend of mine. It kind of gives me hope that maybe I'm not such a loser after all.

Later on we walk in a group to the party, and I stumble a few times on the way there. I'm already drunk. It's at some rundown East Van special, these uniform houses that are cinderblock and poorly constructed. Inside are a bunch people I don't know. Some guy with shaggy red hair that hangs in his face plays a video game.

"Wassup," he says, eyes never leaving the screen. "There's some beer in the fridge."

The room is blue with smoke. Raven and I head to the kitchen, where some people are in the middle of a drinking game at the table. It turns out Raven knows a couple of them.

"Let me play," she says.

"No more joiners," some guys tell her.

"Shut up. Make some room for me and my friend." She picks up the quarter and bounces it into a shot glass.

I sit and watch for a while, taking swigs from a can of beer. Raven warns me, "Maybe you should drink some water. It's not good to switch from coolers to beer."

"Why?" I ask with concern. "Do I look drrrrrunk?" I laugh and then an image of my mom pops into my head, of her lying in that hospital bed with all those rubber tubes sticking out. My stomach rolls and I start to feel queasy.

"I'm gonna get some air," I tell Raven. In the backyard, a couple of guys are smoking a joint and offer me a puff. I sit down on the steps and inhale. Soon I feel funny, buzzed and slightly dizzy. Back inside the living room, the music is thumping. I like the song and start to dance. The beer can is warm in my hand but I finish it anyway.

I don't know how much later it is, but Jesse is dancing with me. His hands are on my ass and I'm aware of how my boobs are pushed up against him. I look around, but I can't see Raven. "Come on, Ariel," he says. "Let's see the East Van two!"

"Show us your tits!"

"You've got nice chestnuts," someone says.

It's such a stupid boy thing to say that I laugh. Suddenly everyone in the room is cheering for me to take off my top, even the girls. I dance a bit, staggering. Then the chanting starts:

"Take it OFF, take it OFF."

In my muddied thinking, it seems I should give my audience what they want, so I pull up my shirt and bra to flash the crowd.

The chorus of male voices howl, "YEEE-AAAAHHHHH!"

All of a sudden someone yanks me backwards. It's Raven, and she drags me toward the front door.

"What the fuck are you doing?" I stumble after her. Then I see the male faces in the crowd. They look like a pack of frenzied dogs, crazed.

For a moment, I'm afraid.

* * *

Raven doesn't say a word the entire way home and stomps ahead of me. I wander by myself, singing half-songs, and every once in awhile she turns around to make sure I'm still there. "You don't have to come with me," I yell.

"You think I'm leaving you in this condition? Forget it."

On the front porch I fumble with my keys. "I'm shorry," I slur. "I'm drunk."

"Save it. There's no point talking to you about anything right now." I know Raven's really mad when I tell her I'll sleep in my mom's bed and she can have my room, but she lies on our lumpy couch and pulls an afghan over her head.

* * *

In the morning I wake to a horrible taste in my mouth that makes me gag. I go to the bathroom and throw up. My hair looks like tangled shrubbery. Even after I brush it out and wash my face, I don't feel much better. I expect Raven to be gone, but she's sitting at the table drinking a mug of tea.

"Good morning," I say weakly.

"Not really," she replies.

"I know. I'm one hot mess."

Raven doesn't let any emotion register on her face. "Don't you care what could have happened to you last night?"

"I was wasted," I say, "hideously drunk." I have a vague memory of raiding the fridge when I got home and biting into a brick of cheese. I open the fridge to check and sure enough, there are tooth marks in the cheddar. "But I barely flashed. And besides —"

"My mom was raped," Raven says. "It happened three years ago."

I freeze. The kitchen is silent except for the ticking clock, and outside the dark sky looks about to storm.

"She was out on the stroll one night. Usually they go out with a partner, but for some reason the other girl wasn't working. A van pulled up and when my mom got inside, someone hit her on the head with a metal pipe and knocked her out. When she woke up they said, 'What's your name?' They said, 'What's the matter, can't talk with a gun in your mouth?'"

I have no idea how to respond. Raven zips up her jacket and slips on her sneakers. "Girls have to watch out for each other," she says.

I'm relieved she's not mad at me anymore, but before leaving she tells me, "You gotta be smart, Ariel. People are already going to think certain things about you. Don't give away your self-respect so easily."

I lock the door after her then go back to sleep for a few hours. When I get up, I make a soup stock then add lentils and vegetables. By the time it's finished cooking, I'm starting to feel human again, and pack some soup into a container for my mom. I walk to Hastings Street and take a bus up Main to Broadway, then walk past city hall and doctors' offices until I reach the hospital. Once again I take the elevator to the seventh floor. My mom sits up, looking better. There is an ancient woman in the bed across from her with a hissing oxygen tube in her nose. My mom makes a big fuss when I arrive.

"I made you some soup," I tell her. "It's really healthy."

"Thank you, honey. I'll just sip the broth. The food here is terrible. At breakfast they gave poor Mrs. Silverman wet toast and salty porridge. Mrs. Silverman," my mom calls, "this is my daughter, Ariel. She made me soup."

"Hello," I say awkwardly because Mrs. Silverman is twirling both fingers in what little hair she has left and looks crazy.

"How precious," Mrs. Silverman says with a gummy smile.

"Just look at this soup," my mom exclaims. She's still doped up so I let her ramble on. "Oh, there's carrots. And celery. Mmmm, lots of garlic. Beans . . ."

"I like beans," says Mrs. Silverman. "Lord knows I do."

My mom's floor houses other people who've had joint replacements. Most of them are in wheelchairs and very old.

"Of course, beans give me terrible gas," Mrs. Silverman continues, "same as cabbage. Oh Lord, it gives me the wind something fierce."

I tell my mom I'm going to get a drink. In the cafeteria, I buy a can of orange juice and finish it while sitting at a table by myself. When I get back to the room, the curtain is drawn around Mrs. Silverman and I can hear her snoring loudly. I still want to ask my mom about Aunt Cathy, but it isn't the time. I get her a fresh jug of water and when I come back, she's dozing, too.

After leaving the hospital, I forget to turn my phone back on. It's late on Sunday night when I listen to a message from Raven. Her voice sounds agitated. "Meet me at the bike racks tomorrow before school," she says. "It's important."

* * *

It seems to takes forever for Raven to walk across

the lot to meet me. Two seniors are standing nearby, laughing at something on their phone. Raven has a hesitant look on her face, and I pull my earphones out. I'm positive she's going to tell me something about Albertine, so I'm confused when she says, "Have you seen it yet?"

"Seen what?"

Raven doesn't even have to answer because the seniors come over to us. "Is this YOU?" one asks, holding out a phone while his friend chortles.

It's me at the party. Someone took a photo when I flashed. My shirt is pulled up to my chin, and my mouth a big sloppy O shape. Also horrific to note is that one eye is half-closed. I look drunk.

"No," I manage. "That's not me." The seniors stumble away, convulsed with laughter.

"Are you going in?" Raven asks.

"There's an Algebra test today," I say numbly. The humiliation is so great I feel like I've been dunked in scalding water.

"I have to go meet with another intake worker." Raven has been trying to get social assistance since she turned nineteen, and the process sometime seems like a part-time job. "I'll come back and pick you up at lunch."

"There's a chance I might not last that long."

Raven waves goodbye and I walk inside. Opening the door I hear kids laughing and right away I assume they're laughing at me. But no one says anything at my locker, and on the way to Biology I wonder if I'm actually going to get through this day. Then I see Kat down the hallway and duck into the girl's bathroom. Before the door closes someone hisses, "SSSSSlut." It's like a cold dagger in the back.

Neville isn't at school, and I sit at my station alone. My iPod is dead, but I put my earphones in anyway. I can hear two girls whispering a few tables over.

"No, that's *her*."

"Omigod, what a skank!"

"I've heard she's had sex with, like, ninety-eight guys! My friend said she's on theNastiness.com."

"Omigod, she probably has an STD."

"I think she *does*."

I get up, loudly banging my stool. The two girls put their hands over their mouths, smirking. I walk to my locker and get my parka. I'll read the chapter in my Biology textbook, and explain to the Algebra teacher that my mom is in the hospital and ask for leniency. But it's my second day skipped, and if I miss one more, they'll start sending letters and calling home.

Leaving school only means I'll have to go back eventually, and it's never really that fun to put off something you dread. The whole walk home I imagine the worst scenarios, knowing I'm forced to return. If I get too far behind, I'll blow my grades and lose any scholarship to help me.

At home, it's quiet like a tomb. I log onto the website the girl mentioned, and it's a shocking sensation when my picture pops up. There I am, in all my drunken toplessness. A shitty cell phone image that will last forever. I don't even look *good*. There is a paragraph accompanying my photo, full of spelling errors and exclamation points:

"this girl is such a slut she had sex with five guys at a party and she always has her tits out cuz that's the only reason guys like her! She screws her friends' boyfriends and wears total stripper clothes to school. She thinks she's so hot but I herd she has herpes stay away from this chick!"

There is a sick feeling in my gut that things are going to get really bad.

Chapter 11

I wonder if those adults who say they were out-casts in high school really have any clue. It means people you don't know believe rumours about you and five guys in a bathroom at a Halloween party. It means you don't have a single friend to talk to all those long, lonely minutes at school, and when the teacher says to find a partner, no one will ever choose you. It means guys you don't know come up and belch in your face. It means that when you try to concentrate in class, you look out the window and long to be far away, to be anywhere but here.

Seven days after surgery, my mom is transferred to a rehabilitation hospital where she will stay for the next two weeks. It's a large, flat complex sur-rounded by level grounds and gardens. In the lobby, people buzz past in motorized wheelchairs. I ask for the room number at the reception area. While the woman behind the desk checks her computer my phone rings. The screen says Unknown Caller.

"Hello?"

"Ariel?

"Yeah."

"This is Julian. Remember me?"

"Yes." The line goes quiet for a moment.

"Are you busy?"

"Miss, no cellular phones are allowed," the receptionist says loudly, pointing to a sign.

"I can't talk," I say. "I'm at the hospital visiting a friend."

"Which one?"

"GF Strong."

"Phones are NOT PERMITTED," the woman barks.

"I've got to go," I say, and hang up. Julian's phone call makes me agitated, but curious, too. The receptionist throws me one last evil glare.

When I get to my mom's room, she's sitting at the desk looking more like her old self. It's a lot nicer here than Vancouver General.

"How's your leg?"

"I can't put weight on it yet," she says, "but when my staples come out, I can start using the pool. We have three physio sessions a day." She asks for the wheelchair outside her door and transfers into it herself.

"Let's go to the day room," she says. I push her down the hall and on the way she introduces me to the nurses. The day room has a nice view and soft chairs. A folding table with a jigsaw puzzle stands in the corner. My mom seems more relaxed now, like the sharpness of the pain she used to feel is gone.

"I'm glad you're doing better," I say.

"I'm lucky that I'll be able to walk again." She tells me the floor above her is for brain and spinal cord injuries. "All those boys upstairs have tragic stories. One young man snapped his neck doing mountain bike jumps. Another was dragged a hundred yards by a drunken woman's car."

"That's terrible," I say and mean it. My chin is already down on the floor.

"What's wrong, Ariel? You don't look well."

"I'm just tired."

"Are you having a hard time on your own? Do you want someone to come and stay with you?"

"No, it's fine. I'm just having some problems with school stuff. What if I finished the term at another school?"

"You want to transfer schools? What's going on?"

"Nothing is going *on*. Its just, y'know, not a very good school."

"It's your decision," she says, but I can see a big worry line crease between her eyebrows.

"Forget it," I say. "It's nothing, honestly. Tell me some more about these people on the other floors. Did you meet them at lunch or something?"

"Yes, we all eat in the cafeteria together. The food is actually quite good. One boy had been riding on top of a train and didn't make a tunnel," she continues. "Oh, and this poor man had a stroke and his wife asked him for a divorce in the hospital."

"That's terrible," I say, but my mind is racing with ways to get out of school tomorrow.

"People who deal with constant pain have tremendous power —"

"Mom," I interrupt without really thinking. "Did you keep the flowers?"

"Which flowers?'

"That big bouquet from Uncle Jack and Aunt Cathy."

"Oh, I left that at the hospital for other people to enjoy."

"The first night I came to visit, you said something about Cathy being mad at you. Is that why she never sees us anymore?"

My mom pulls her sweater closed. I know how she feels about people who tell lies. She puts her hands in her lap and looks at me. "Yes, she refused to speak to me for the past year or so."

"Did you have an affair with Uncle Jack?" The words are like lead. A nurse walks in, looks at my trembling face, then turns around.

"I'll come back," she says, closing the door.

"It happened only once, years ago," my mom says quietly. "And it was after your father died."

"How could you do that to Aunt Cathy?"

"It was grief, Ariel. After I lost your dad, I couldn't bear it. For some reason it came up last year. She'd never asked me about it before, so I never had to lie."

"You always say an omission is the same as a

lie. Of course she never visits anymore!" I yell. "It's because of YOU."

I can tell my mom is upset. Her voice shakes when she says, "Everyone makes mistakes."

"Okay, great," I say. "Thanks for the top-notch parenting. No wonder people call me a skank. Look at my role model." I grab my coat and fly out of the room.

"Ariel!" my mom exclaims. "Let's talk about this."

Someone holds the elevator, and the last thing I see is my mom trying to wheel herself down the hallway. "ARIEL, wait!"

The elevator doors close and I can still hear her calling. Outside, I run all the way to the bus stop and then try to catch my breath. The sky rumbles and pours rain. After a twenty-minute wait, the bus comes by with a "Sorry. Full" sign. The next one is out of service. I curse and start walking in the downpour. I can't stay in the same place any longer. Then a car rolls up alongside me.

I'm at my lowest point ever when I see the metallic green Cadillac with fins. It's waiting for me, engine idling. Julian rolls down the passenger-side window.

"Hey, pretty girl," he says.

It can't be a random coincidence that Julian's shown up. His black pompadour is back in place along with his big showman's grin.

"What are you doing here?"

"I happened to be nearby when we spoke." That's weird, since the rehab hospital is pretty far out, but I'm shivering, and he says, "Ariel, you're soaked. Let me give you a ride."

I hesitate. Something doesn't feel right, but it's a long walk home. "Ariel," he calls softly. "Get in." And I do.

The car has the fine smell of new leather, and the interior is polished to a gleam. The dashboard lights give off a strange light and fuzzy dice hang from the rearview mirror. I give them a vicious swat.

"You're in a mood, girl." He pulls into traffic. "Heading downtown?"

"Sure."

"Who were you visiting? Someone close?"

"Yes," I answer curtly. It is clearly not a topic open for discussion.

Julian turns up the car stereo and taps his hand on the steering wheel to the rockabilly beats. There are big silver rings on his fingers. Despite my lousy day, it feels cool riding in this Cadillac, and I notice how people at stoplights take notice of us.

"You look good in this car," he laughs. "But you'd look good in anything."

We veer into the lane going across one of the bridges that lead toward the skyscrapers of downtown. The lights of Granville Island reflect off the water in the inlet and from the glass towers looming larger as we approach. I could be anyone right now, a complete stranger in this landscape, riding in this car. I could be anyone that's not me.

"Thanks for the lift."

"It seems like you're having a bad day."

I look over at Julian and our eyes meet. With his leather jacket and pompadour, I picture him in a three-piece band playing a stand-up bass. I have no idea how old he is, or if he knows I'm in high school.

"Things are kind of rough right now," I say. "I'm dealing with a lot."

"Tell me."

"Why? It won't make life any easier. I just want to leave this whole city."

"So go away for a while and come back when things blow over."

"Sure," I say looking at my reflection in the window. "Easier said than done."

"Do you live alone?"

"Yes," I answer truthfully. "Right now I do."

Julian stops at another red light. "Left or right?" he asks. Granville Street ends in the middle of a dense tourist area lined with fast food restaurants, bars, and dance clubs. A left turn will take us past the expensive boutiques on Robson Street, into the largely gay West End. Going right will head into Gastown and finally the lower east side.

"I can just get out here."

Julian stops me as I reach for the door handle. "How about we have a drink?"

I imagine ordering in a plush bar and the waitress asking for my ID. "I don't feel like going out," I say.

"How about coming to my place? It's not far."

I'd rather go anywhere than home right now.

"Alright," I agree. "But I'm only having one." And I mean it. The drunken photograph of me is not something easily forgotten.

"My place it is," he says, turning the wheel.

* * *

Julian lives in a luxury apartment just blocks from the Granville Street bridge. When he pulls into the underground parking, it takes two different pass keys to get to the lobby. There is a security guard and a doorman in a hat and tailored coat to greet us. We ride the elevator to the seventh floor, the same number my mom was on at VGH. The image of her struggling to chase me in her wheelchair makes me feel like a real creep. Inside Julian's apartment, my feet sink into the thick white carpet. The ceiling-high windows offer a spectacular panoramic view.

"This is amazing," I say, checking out the room. Julian comes out of the kitchen with a bottle of wine and pulls the cork out with flair. He pours two glasses and hands one to me. I feel very grown up. Then he asks the question I've been waiting to hear.

"How old are you?"

"Eighteen," I lie smoothly.

One entire wall is covered in artistic black and white photographs of nude women. I stand and gaze at them for a while. They all look so beautiful and glamorous. Comparing my own topless photo makes me cringe. It's hard to believe how much

117

has happened to me in just one day. Julian walks out onto the balcony. The rain has stopped, and he tells me to join him. Surrounding us are the windows of other buildings and I can look right into a bunch of apartments. Most of them are dark except for a TV flickering.

"Can you imagine how many people out there are having sex right now?"

"Probably a lot." I blush.

The wind is chilly so I go back inside and sit down on one of the soft leather couches. Julian shuts the balcony doors and lights a fire. The wine is making me feel warm and my thinking is fuzzy. All the garbage at school and Kat and the fight with my mother seems very far away.

"Have you ever thought about being a model?"

"No," I say self-consciously. "Well, this woman gave me a card once for her agency. I made my mom take me there, but they said I was too top-heavy."

"That couldn't possibly be true."

"No, it is," I insist, turning to face him. I don't feel self conscious at all anymore. "These things are *heavy*. I get really bad backaches. I'm always hunched over."

It's weird to be telling a guy this, but Julian makes it easy to talk to him. He pours us both more wine, and my eyes wander back to the wall of nude photographs.

I ask, "Did you take all of these?"

"Yes. I have a studio I work out of in Gastown. But some of them were shot right here."

My mind flashes again to my topless photo. Half my school has probably seen it by now. As if reading my thoughts, Julian says, "I could make you look just as good. You have fantastic bone structure."

"Well, people do love to take my picture," I answer dryly.

"C'mon," he says. "It'll be fun." I sip my glass of wine while Julian hangs up a black cloth for a backdrop and adjusts the lighting. Then he positions me in front of the camera and says all I have to do is stand there.

He turns the music louder and begins with head shots. "Gorgeous," he says from behind the camera. At first I just stand awkwardly, but he encourages me to move around, praising every angle. I relax and start to have fun. "Okay, now let's open that top button . . . another one, yes . . . beautiful, great, great, great." Julian instructs me in a couple of different poses and keeps snapping. Then he lowers the camera.

"How about making things a little more interesting?"

"What do you mean?"

He gives a boyish laugh. "I was just thinking you could lose the top."

"I don't know . . ."

"No one would see these images except me," Julian says. "I promise."

There are warning bells in my head. It's ridiculous to consider another topless photo after my current fiasco, but I think, *it's out there already*.

Julian lights a cigarette and streams smoke toward the ceiling. Then he opens his wallet and pulls out a stack of twenties, counting them off. The pile looks like a lot of money. He gets behind the lens again and points in my direction. "You are so unbelievably hot," he says.

It's easy to go too far when someone makes you feel good.

* * *

I check the number before opening my phone. "Hey Raven," I answer.

"I've found Albertine. Can you meet me at my place?"

"I'm in Gastown," I say. "Give me fifteen minutes."

I gather my things together to leave. In the front pocket of my jeans the wad of money makes an accusatory bulge. Julian hands me another business card at the door. "Give me your email address and I'll send you some of the photos. We should start working on a portfolio for you. I think you could do really well in this business."

"I don't have a computer," I say. "Well, not one you could send those photos to."

"Hold on," Julian says, and goes into another room. He comes back with a thin silver laptop and hands it to me. "It's a gift."

"You're giving this laptop to me?"

"I've got a box of them."

"Is this stolen?"

"No," Julian answers. "But let's put it this way — I got it on the *grey* market."

"Uh, thanks." Already I'm thinking of a way to explain this to my mom.

"It's got a built-in web cam. We can talk to each other online."

I put the laptop in my backpack with the cords and Julian walks me to the elevator door. He brushes my hair aside and gives me a gentle kiss on the forehead. Downstairs, the doorman winks and tips his hat as I head out into the cold night air.

Chapter 12

I'm walking so fast it doesn't take me long to get to Raven's. I feel vulnerable with all that money in my pocket. There are dirty puddles on the sidewalk and my sneakers squish on the wet cement.

Raven is outside her building waiting for me. She's got a skateboard in her hand and taps her leg relentlessly. "Someone told my mom they saw Albertine working a block near the railroad tracks on Powell. Down by the old sugar refinery."

"Is Netti coming, too?"

"No." Raven doesn't elaborate. "Let's go to your house and get your bike." My crappy old ten-speed will make our mission faster, and I'm glad to drop off my backpack with the laptop. In my room, I push the handful of twenties to the bottom of my underwear drawer.

We follow the railroad tracks down Powell Street and cruise block after block. There's no sign of Albertine. The only woman working is middle-aged with gigantic breasts. Raven stops to ask her, "Have you seen my sister?" Once again she unfolds the wrinkled photocopy from her back pocket. The woman checks the photo and shakes her head. She's got thick glasses and short hair, and looks like someone's grandmother.

The rusty chain on my ten-speed groans as I pedal beside Raven. "Let's try the women's shelter," she says. We head back to the heart of the Downtown Eastside, and I wait outside with my bike while Raven goes in to check. As the door swings open and shut I see a big room full of women sitting or laying on cots. A few are talking but most of them look depressed, beaten-down. There are huge signs posted everywhere: NO MEN ALLOWED.

A small woman with a ball cap comes out and says, "Donations? You got any donations?" She's missing her front teeth and her eyes are brilliant with laughter.

Raven storms back outside. "She's not here. I'm so frustrated right now I could scream!"

"Donations?"

"NO!"

"Let's go get some coffee," I tell Raven. "We need a new strategy."

We're a few blocks from Chinatown, and I push my bike alongside her. It's getting close to midnight, but we find a restaurant that's nearly empty and slide into a booth. The wine at Julian's has made me sleepy. A yellowing menu is placed before us, and a moment later another waiter appears at our table to take the order. Then Raven calls Netti.

"Hey, it's me. No, I didn't see her. Someone gave you bad information. I'll keep looking. I can't, I'm with Ariel right now. Okay, bye."

Raven hands me back my phone. "Netti thanks you."

"I just hope you find your sister."

"A lot of women go missing down here," Raven says darkly. "One day they stop picking up their welfare cheques or just leave their apartments and never come back. No one does anything about it."

Our soup comes, a big watery bowl of broth and a few limp vegetables. Neither one of us have an appetite. "Someone put my photo on a gossip site," I tell her.

"I know. I wasn't sure if you'd heard."

"What they wrote on it is pretty harsh."

"Kat?"

"Probably."

"You can file a civil suit against her," Raven says. "It's slander. I read about how a woman got a hundred thousand dollars for that."

"Really? I'll get my lawyer right on it," I say.

The waiter comes with a plate of fried rice. We pick at it listlessly. "How's your mom?" Raven asks.

"I just saw her at the rehab hospital. We had a fight." I spear a mushroom with my chopstick.

"Why?"

"It's nothing." I shrug. I don't want to tell anyone

about my mom's affair with Uncle Jack. "I'm just upset about all that other shit."

"No kidding," Raven says.

I blurt, "I got a ride home from the hospital with this guy Julian."

"Who's that?"

"Actually, you saw him once. Remember getting gelato the first day we met? You thought he was hitting on me. It turns out his runs this company called Vixen Media."

"That guy driving the green Caddy?"

"Yeah. He gave me a laptop."

"What do you mean? Were you at his place? Is that where you were when I called?"

She gets so upset I start to feel defensive. "Yes," I admit.

"And he just *gave* you a laptop. You didn't have to do anything for it."

"Uh . . . yeah."

Raven can tell I'm lying, and her spoon drops in disgust. I ask, "Why? What do you know about him?"

"Vixen Media makes porn, you idiot. He probably wants you to be a web-cam girl or something. I also heard they've got some place that's wired with hidden cameras and they bring girls there to film. That guy's so sleazy, Ariel. Can't you tell that? Whatever you're thinking of doing . . . DON'T."

"I would never," I hear myself say weakly. The smiling waiter comes by with the bill.

"Bullshit. I don't believe you. He probably said you could make a lot of money."

"He did," I finally say. "What's the big deal? My life isn't exactly a big bucket of rainbows right now."

"So you're gonna go ahead and make it worse?"

I shrug, and Raven slams her palms down on the table. "There are girls out there working on the street who've been *abused*. Or they have some kind of mental problem, or their mother was a drug addict so they become drug addicts, too. They don't have many choices. But here you are with this great mom, and this beautiful face and brains . . ."

"My mom isn't that great," I interrupt.

". . . but you're gonna give everything up to flash your tits for the rest of your life. Well, good luck with that. They won't last forever, y'know."

"Raven, don't get mad at me."

"I'm not mad," she snaps. "I've just got too many problems to deal with yours right now."

The wine sloshes around my stomach. I sit and listen to the din of chattering customers as Raven slides out of the booth, tossing a few coins on the table. "See you around," she says. The bell on the door dings and then she's gone.

* * *

For the next two weeks I only go to classes now and then. The day before my mom is due to come home, I take myself shopping. My first stop is the store that sold the leather jacket I had seen at Christmas. The jacket is still there, and I try it on again. It makes me look tough, a little more invincible. At the counter, the cashier doesn't bat an eye when I pay for it with a stack of twenties. I put it on and strut all the way home.

The next afternoon, the Handi-Dart drops my mom off in front of the house. I come outside to help her. "It's so good to be home. I've missed you, sweetie," she says, trying to hug me while balancing on her crutches. I pick up her bags and follow her inside.

I feel even worse because I haven't seen her once since our fight. We've talked on the phone, but I always had an excuse why I couldn't come to visit. She drops her crutches and sinks onto the couch.

"Do you need anything?" I ask. "There's a lot of homework I have to do."

My mom arranges herself on the pillows. "Yes, you seem to be quite busy with school lately."

"Yeah, I was," I answer. "I am. Not to mention buying groceries, cleaning the house, and doing laundry."

"Thank you, my love." My mom leans back and closes her eyes.

"And I made spaghetti sauce. It's on the stove." She doesn't answer, so I go to my bedroom and close the door. In a little while I hear snoring coming from the living room, so I pull out my laptop and start surfing the web. I lose track of time and then my mom knocks and opens my door, startling me.

"Where did you get that?"

"What?"

"Don't be coy, Ariel. I'm referring to the brand new laptop. Is that from Uncle Jack?"

"It belongs to a friend."

"Who?"

"You don't know him. I'm just borrowing it," I say. "He's got more."

"Ariel, please don't lie to me."

"Hey, you're the secret-keeper in *this* family," I spit. "So what, this guy likes to give me presents. Isn't that what Uncle Jack does for you?"

"I'm sorry —"

"Don't worry," I say, cutting her off. "Everyone makes mistakes, right? Life is just one big series of them. So you make yours and I'll make mine."

My mom lets out a disappointed sigh and lurches out of the room on her crutches. Right now I officially feel like the world's worst daughter. I shut the door and lie on the bed. A chat window pops up on my computer. It's Julian.

All it says is, "Thinking about you."

A minute later, my phone receives a text from Julian. When I open the message there are no words, just one of my topless photos.

I put my earphones on and turn the music up to drown out any thoughts that might creep in.

* * *

The next morning, I wake early and leave the house before my mom is even up. Instead of going to Algebra class, I sit in the library and stare at my laptop. It's so much easier to ignore people with technology. But as I'm walking down the hall, someone kicks me from behind. It's Kat, with her skunk streaks and heavy makeup. Her mouth is pursed in a sour line which opens to say, "Watch it, you dumb skank."

Something just takes over me. My books drop as I lunge at her, feel my fingernails dig into her flesh. Kat is up against the wall and I hold her there, arms trembling. Up close I see she's got bad skin under that layer of cover-up. I've never noticed that before. Kids gather around us cheering.

"Chick fight!" some guy yells. I let go of her and push my way through the crowd.

"Oh my god, what a FREAK," Kat shrieks. "Did everyone see that?"

I walk into Journalism class and tell Mr. Yaworski I have to go home and take care of my mom, who just got out of the hospital.

"Ariel, you've missed quite a few classes lately."

"She's really sick." I lean over the desk so my top spills open.

Mr. Yaworski clears his throat. "Alright," he says. "Just leave. I'll inform the office."

Outside, I walk all the way to the Skytrain station and buy a ticket. The ride goes past the giant orb of Science World and BC Place stadium. I get off and browse in a few stores and use some of my remaining money to treat myself to a nice lunch. Then I buy a killer pair of heels and a new bag. It's easy to get used to money. It may not solve all your problems, but for a while it can help you forget they exist. The sun comes out and I walk most of the way home, stretching out my new heels. It's been such a pleasant day that I'm mildly shocked when I open the door and my mom begins to yell.

"Where were you today? The school called. They've said you've missed *numerous* days. They want me to come in for a meeting. You might even be suspended!"

"I missed a few days. What's the big deal?"

"Skipping school while I was in the hospital? Ariel, I expected better from you."

"Well, I expected better from YOU," I yell. I'm not even that mad about her and Uncle Jack, but it feels good to scream. "I'm sick of living in this shit hole. I'm sick of this LIFE!"

My mom blinks her eyes, and I can tell she's holding back tears. "Why are you lashing out like this?"

"If they suspend me, that's just fine," I say. "But don't expect me to go back."

"You are *not* quitting school. Whatever problems there are can be dealt with."

"How can you stop me?" I ask. "I'll be eighteen next year and then I can do whatever the hell I want." My jacket is still on and I race outside, slamming the door. But as I stomp down the street I realize I have nowhere to go. I try Dina and Tish, but neither pick up. We haven't talked since Christmas. I'm truly alone in the world. I pull the business card from my wallet and dial. Julian answers.

"Come over," he says.

Chapter 13

Julian isn't at his apartment, so he gives me directions to his studio loft near the steam clock in Gastown. Around me, the last of the tourists rush to the safety of their hotel rooms before the real action starts. The address is one of the new, expensively renovated buildings and there's a title by the buzzer that says, "Vixen Media, Inc."

"Second floor," Julian says over the intercom. He buzzes me in.

The lobby is concrete and steel. Aside from a lightbox on one wall, it's very cold and impersonal. I walk up the stairs and the second floor door slides open.

"Hey, baby girl," Julian says. He gives me a kiss on each cheek, European-style. "You're as gorgeous as ever. Come on in."

The space in the loft is the opposite of Julian's apartment. Though the ceilings are high, the windows are blacked out, and there's no furniture except for a couch and coffee table. All the walls are bare. There are, however, some lights set up around a huge bed. Julian invites me to sit on the couch, and gives an affectionate pat on my shoulder.

"Are you having a bad day?" He talks to me like I'm a house cat or something.

"I'm having the *worst* day," I tell him. Right now I don't even care what his motives might be. I just need a friendly face.

"How can I help?"

Tears begin to well as I shake my head. "You can't. Trust me."

"Okay, then," Julian says, "how about a drink?"

After a few minutes, he comes back and hands me a glass with orange juice. The liquid burns down my throat and I shudder. "Tequila," he laughs.

"So, this is your studio?"

"Vixen Media happens right here."

I blurt out, "My friend told me you guys make porn movies."

But Julian doesn't hesitate. "It's a legitimate company. We even advertise in the Georgia Straight."

The Georgia Straight is the free newspaper in town that has lame interviews and reviews. It's like a Zellers flyer with entertainment listings. "Well, that's not too impressive."

Julian laughs. "You're a sharp one, Ariel. Listen, I showed a couple of people your photos. They were *extremely* impressed."

"You said those were for personal use."

He keeps talking like I haven't spoken. "We agree there's a lot of money you could make on film. A girl like you could get fifteen hundred, maybe two grand for a day's work."

I'm not ready for any of this. "Can I use your bathroom?" I need more than a minute to get myself together. On the edge of the giant marble tub I put my hands on my knees and take a few deep breaths. The shower has three Plexiglas walls around it, and I wonder if Julian uses it to shoot porn scenes, like Raven said. On impulse, I open one of the cupboards under the sink. There's an enema bag inside, and I quickly shut the door.

"Are you okay?" Julian asks as I come down the hallway. My drink is refilled on the coffee table.

"I'm not interested," I say firmly. "You promised you wouldn't show those photos to anyone. I should probably go."

"Don't," Julian says with a pleasant smile. "We won't talk about it again. At least finish your drink."

I sit down and take another swallow. It leaves a salty taste in my mouth. "Tequila isn't my favourite," I say politely, even though it's the first time I've tasted it.

Julian starts talking about some car show he plans to drive to in Long Beach, California, and invites me to come along. I imagine the hot sun and ocean waves, and then a feeling of deep relaxation comes over me, with a rush of euphoria that gives me a big gooey smile. Every muscle loosens and I sink even further into the couch. It seems perfectly natural to close my eyes. Julian keeps chatting.

But then my skin starts to feel warm. I'm too hot and tug at my sweater. "Don't feel good," I mumble. I want to get up, but my limbs feel made of concrete. Behind my eyelids, everything spins like the amusement park ride that goes around and around as gravity suspends you.

"Maybe you should lie down." I hear Julian's voice, but it sounds distorted and very far away. Hands grab my arms and pull me up. I manage to open my eyes and it's like I'm looking through a lens smeared with Vaseline. My muscles give an involuntary twitch. I can't even form words.

Then my eyes close again and I fall into a long black tunnel with no end.

Chapter 14

The first thing I realize is that my feet are very cold. There is cool air on my face and raindrops falling. Hands are shaking me.

"Ariel," a woman's voice says. "Wake up, little one, wake up."

Someone is lightly slapping my face. I open my eyes in a daze and realize the hands on me are Netti's. It's still dark outside and I have no concept of how much time has passed. My muscles are so cramped I can barely move, and it takes me a minute to realize I'm propped in the corner of a bus shelter. My freezing feet are bare.

"Someone took my shoes," I mumble.

My purse is gone too, and Netti searches my pockets, finding my phone. I can hear her talking, but can't make out all the words.

"Found her . . . East Cordova . . . don't know."

Then Netti sits downs beside me and pulls me

close, rubbing my arms to warm me up. She whispers soothing words in a language I don't understand. My body aches all over and I close my eyes again.

* * *

When I wake up I'm on Netti's couch. There is a horrible oily taste in my mouth and I stumble to the bathroom to retch. Netti is there in an instant, patting my back, offering more kindness than I can bear.

"Please don't," I manage.

She leaves the bathroom and shuts the door. I stare at myself in the mirror. My face is deathly pale and under my eyes are smears of mascara. No wonder I wasn't bothered on the bus bench. With my rumpled clothes and matted hair I look homeless and deranged.

This makes me giggle. I laugh so hard I can't breathe, even though nothing about this is funny. Raven comes barrelling into the bathroom.

"Are you okay? Oh my god, what happened?" She is almost frantic. "My mom found you passed out in a bus shelter in the middle of the night! Do you have any idea what could have happened to you?"

"Julian," I begin, before I lean over the toilet and throw up again.

"You were with Julian? Did he do something to you?"

The entire night, from the glass of tequila and orange juice to Netti waking me up is a thick fog.

"I can't remember," I say. "I really can't."

I start to cry, and it doesn't seem like it will ever stop.

I come back to life on a soiled couch in a run-down apartment in the worst part of town. Slowly we piece the story together. Netti had been walking home and saw me in the bus shelter, only half a block from Julian's studio. He'd dumped me out on the corner when he was done. When I say this Raven makes a garbled sound of rage and starts pounding on a wall with her fist. My legs are wobbling, but I get up and stop her.

"I never should have trusted him," I say.

"It's not your fault. You're a seventeen-year-old girl and he's a piece of shit."

"That's right," Netti says.

"You have to tell the cops about him," Raven says, but I'm not ready to deal with that yet. I don't want the world to know about the naked photos I let him take, or anything that came afterwards. But I think how Julian pretended to care, then put me out on the corner like a bag of garbage. We decide to make an anonymous call.

The hours until morning are spent tossing, queasy and sick. I wake up tucked under an afghan. The room is filled with weak sunshine creeping under the blinds. My first thought that breaks with the light is that I want to go home and see my mom.

There's a lot I have to tell her.

Epilogue

It's a hot, spring day in Oppenheimer Park. Raven and I stand arm in arm. On the other side of me is my mom. Netti is there, too, along with Raven's aunties. It's a Memorial for all the missing women on the lower east side. People are holding candles, and after a drum ceremony, the women's names are called out. It's a very long list. Raven and Netti both hold pictures of Albertine. As I stand with them, I reflect how the last year of my life hasn't been easy, and even now it feels surreal, like it happened in someone else's dream. But compared to these missing women, and the anguish of their families who gather here, my problems don't seem as enormous.

Then the ceremony is over and the crowd begins to break up. There are Native women in traditional clothing, girls riding BMX's, and elderly ladies leaning on each other. Sex trade workers, homeless women, hippie chicks, tough rockers, mothers holding their children. We're all just kind of meandering together.

"Any news about the trial?" Raven asks.

After Julian was taken into custody, he got out on bail right away, and is trying to have the charges dropped. My lawyer warns that in court they will bring up that I lied about my age, and that I went to his place voluntarily. But the police found the photos of me on his computer when they searched his apartment, and there's no argument against that kind of evidence. Being a minor, my name was kept out of the papers. Julian is prohibited from ever contacting me again. His green Cadillac isn't on the streets, but some days I expect to see it around every corner.

"He got a continuance again."

"Money can buy everything, eh?"

"Not everything," I answer. I pull out my phone and check the time. "Damn, my shift starts in an hour."

I only pretend to be annoyed, because I really love my job. I work in a vintage store for a woman named Trixie. She's a loud, pot-bellied Turk who left Istanbul with her small sons in the early eighties. The shop is called Bazaar and sells everything from clothing, fabric, suitcases, and records, to ornaments, tea sets, and Persian rugs. Sometimes Trixie sends me to garage sales and flea markets to buy stuff that she jacks up the price on and re-sells. She says it's too bad if wealthy people are too stupid to know better. I've been hired for weekend shifts because Trixie has a cabaret act she performs with two peacocks and sleeps until late in the day.

"I'm going back to Rupert again." Raven will stay restless until she finds Albertine. She'll never stop searching.

"How long will you be gone?"

"I'm not sure this time."

A lot has happened in a few months. My mom and I had a meeting with the principal and I got a tutor for Algebra. She says I can spend two weeks in New York this summer with Uncle Jack and Aunt Cathy, if I pass all my classes. Now I see a therapist twice a week, too. Her name is Dr. Reagan but I call her Angela. It helps to have her to talk to, and she's teaching me ways to cope with what I've been through. It's not like things at school changed overnight, but the insults began to fall away. Or maybe they bothered me less because I stopped paying attention.

One day I caught Katrina Kubalowski crying in the girl's can. She'd been sitting alone at lunch hour all week, usually hunched over her tray. I was washing my hands and heard stifled sobs. When Kat's red, puffy face emerged from the stall, our eyes locked in the mirror. She twisted her mouth into a sneer. I simply asked, "Are you okay?" Her face crumpled. I saw how she was just a scared, insecure girl like the rest of us. She didn't seem like such a formidable enemy anymore. Being able to show her decency was a bigger victory than seeing her picked on like I used to be.

I watch my mom who is chatting with Netti, then look at all the people around me, the ones who make up my neighbourhood. There's so much desperation here, but also courage and fight. I finally get how I am more than what other people think of me. I can't be defined only by my mistakes, or where I live, or my bra size. The world is open to me for anything.

Raven asks, "You gonna be able to finish this high school crap without me?"

"I'll survive," I answer. And then I think,
Hell yeah.

Read more great teen fiction from SideStreets.

Ask for them at your local library, bookstore, or order them online at www.lorimer.ca.

Skin Deep
By Sandra Diersch

School's out for summer and Corinne and Romi have big plans for a transformation that will put them at the top of next year's A-list. At least that was the plan, until Corinne's mom's secret threatens to ruins Cori's summer, and maybe even her life.
ISBN: 978-1-55277-474-8 (paperback)

Thief Girl
By Ingrid Lee

Avvy Go straddles the line — the line between the immigrant neighbourhood where she lives and works and the established neighbourhood where she goes to high school, the line between right and wrong, and the line between telling secrets and keeping them . . .
ISBN: 978-1-55277-538-7 (paperback)

Last Chance
By Lesley Choyce

"You can't stay around this scene. I've seen what it does to kids. Girls become merchandise." Melanie's determined not to let that happen to her. She may be on the street, but as long as she has Trent, she still has hope.
ISBN: 978-1-55277-444-1 (paperback)

Ceiling Stars
By Sandra Diersch

Christine and Danelle have been friends FOREVER. Danelle's always been the wacky one, pushing 'Prissy Chrissy' to loosen up, to have some real fun. But now Christine's scared — Danelle's ideas go way beyond fun. How far will Christine go to make her best friend happy?

ISBN: 978-1-55028-834-6 (paperback)

Every Move
By Peter McPhee

Emily looked down at the present from Michael in her hands. "This isn't sweet. It's psycho." At first Emily's flattered — what girl wouldn't want two guys chasing her? But when Emily chooses Daniel over Michael, Michael can't seem to take the hint and get lost. That's when things start to get really creepy.

ISBN: 978-1-55028-850-6 (paperback)

On the Game
By Monique Polak

Yolande heard Richie remove a condom from its foil wrapper. She remembered what Etienne had told her: "Just make him happy." Was this what he meant? Etienne is older that Yolande, and he's hot. He showers her with gifts, tells her how beautiful she is, and lavishes attention on her. And she'll do anything she can to keep him.

ISBN: 978-1-55028-876-6 (paperback)

Scarred
By Monique Polak

A Failure. Disappointment. Her mom doesn't have to say it out loud — Becky knows she's thinking it, and it's making Becky feel numb, disconnected. If she can just cut deep enough, the voice inside her head tells her, maybe she'll finally feel alive again.
ISBN: 978-1-55028-964-0 (paperback)

Klepto
By Lori Weber

Kat's parents couldn't be happier: soon her older sister Hannah will be coming home from a place for troubled teens. But as her sister's homecoming gets closer, what started as a harmless rush for Kat becomes a dangerous addiction she can't control.
ISBN: 978-1-55028-836-0 (paperback)

Tattoo Heaven
By Lori Weber

As if it weren't bad enough that Jackie's dad walked out on them, he left for a younger woman. Jackie's mom reacts like it's a "fresh new start" and busies herself by getting a job and some hobbies, leaving Jackie alone to pick up the pieces of her shattered family.
ISBN: 978-1-55028-902-2 (paperback)